IN THE PAST

IN THE PAST

BY

E M ELLIOT

For Allan

who has always believed in me

Chapter One

Katherine Muier gazed at the wreck in front of her and, not for the first time, wondered whether she had done the right thing. Wynenden Farm was a traditional Kentish Farmhouse which consisted of a brick base, white weatherboarding and a Kent Peg Tile roof. Currently covered in brambles and ivy which had cunningly, and sneakily, weaved their way through any little cracks they could find, searching for ways into the house. Persistence had paid off, ivy had crept in so successfully that it had created a wallpaper effect in parts of the interior; an absolute nightmare for any house as it eroded brickwork, and set about its domination determinedly. That, along with the leaking roof, collapsed ceiling in parts of the house, rustic wiring and atrocious plumbing, meant that the house was in need of some serious TLC.

Katherine had purchased the house from the Wynenden Park Estate owned by Sir Geoffrey Percevall-Sharparrow. It had been empty for more than thirty years, Katherine had stumbled across it, and its five acres, when out for a walk one bright spring day. Now, a surprisingly swift six months later, she had just completed on the property and the reality of what she had done hit her like a slap in the face. She leant back against the rickety gate, only to stagger backwards when its rotten timbers gave way. Composing herself, she gingerly picked her way through the long grass, keeping as much to the path trodden down by her surveyor, architect and builder on their numerous visits, as possible.

Pushing aside her panic attack of fears, she did her best to immerse herself in her usual positive, bright and cheery self, and retrieved the cumbersome iron key to the front door from her rucksack. Fiddling around to get it into just the right position to open the door, she smiled with satisfaction as it gave a heavy clunk into place, and turned the key creakily in the lock. As quickly as the wave of panic had hit her moments before, a frisson of excitement buzzed inside her. This was it, this was hers, she almost couldn't believe it. She shoved the door with her shoulder to open it, swollen by years of neglect and the dampness of the autumn season, even the warmth of the October day failing to have any effect. As usual, she was hit by the damp, mushroomy smell, which escaped in a rush each time the door was open. Her tall, skinny figure stooped slightly under the door frame to enter in. She stopped and listened, silence, and then faintly, the drip, drip, drip of one of the many leaks.

'Hi Kitty,' called a cheery voice from behind her, making her jump. It was Dougie Brown her builder who, like many, automatically called her Kitty, rather than Katherine, she could never fathom out why some people she met called her by her school nickname from the offset. He was a short, round, jolly fellow in his mid-fifties, with a huge smile that filled his chubby face, and a messy mop of grey hair. Her 5'9" towered over his 5'5", but what he lacked in height, he made up for in personality. She'd never seen him grumpy, but a cynical part of her thought that perhaps this was due to the huge profit he would be making out of the restoration of her house, if the figures he'd presented her with were anything to go by.

'Hi Dougie, how are you?'

'Grand, just grand.' He smiled, rubbing his hands together. 'So, where do you want to start?' He was here to go through, one final time, the schedule of works, before they started on site the following week.

'Page one and work our way through I suppose.'

They progressed their way through the two reception rooms, the jumble of smaller rooms at the back, which would be knocked into one large kitchen/breakfast room, and were upstairs going through the four bedrooms, other rooms which would become two bathrooms, and the loft area, when they were interrupted by the one voice which set Katherine's heckles rising – Andrew Battle.

'Kitty, looking as lovely as ever,' he oozed giving her, what he thought, was his most seductive, and winning smile.

'Andrew.' She pulled a taught smile in response. Her gold-flecked brown eyes narrowed suspiciously at him. She knew what was coming, and wished he'd leave her alone. Dougie stood behind her, his arms crossed firmly across his chest, and scowled at Andrew. He too knew what Andrew was after.

Andrew continued, seemingly oblivious to the hostility facing him. 'Just picked the keys up then?'

'Yes.'

'Complete wreck, isn't it? Far too much to do. You really don't want to be worrying your pretty little head about something like this. An enchanting woman like you must be far too busy to bother with this sort of project?' He tilted his head slightly to one side, and gave her a knowing look with his piercing blue eyes.

I think I want to slap him, thought Katherine, and I do wish he'd stop calling me Kitty, far too over familiar for a Lothario like him. 'Actually, Andrew, it's exactly what I need, and what I have spent my whole life looking forward to, taking on a project like this.' All 47 years of them she thought to herself.

'OK. OK. Tell you what. I will add another ten percent to my offer price, how about that? Can't say fairer than that. I'll take it off your hands. Won't take my solicitor long to get the paperwork sorted. How about it?' His smile seemed pleasant, but Katherine could see the hardness in his eyes.

She sighed, and was glad that Dougie was beside her, coiled like a stubby spring ready to pounce and remove the irritation from her house. 'Andrew.' He smiled encouragingly back at her. 'Let me make this absolutely clear one last time. I do *not*, and *never will*, want to sell this house. And if, in many years to come, I should change my mind and want to sell it, I will never. Do you hear? NEVER. Sell the house to you. Do I make myself absolutely clear?' she glared at him.

He stared deeply at her, the air bristling with animosity from him. Quietly, almost imperceptibly, he replied. 'You're making a mistake Kitty, a *big* mistake. I will get this house, whether you like it or not.' He swung round, and strode arrogantly out of the room. His back stiff in his tailored shirt, the diamonds on his watch flashing furiously. They listened in silence, until they heard the roar of one of his many high performance cars, screech off up the lane.

Katherine shivered. 'Did he just threaten me?'

'Pay no attention to him. The house is legally yours, there's nothing he can do. He likes to throw his weight around, expects to get his own way, and throws his toys out of his pram if he doesn't. Now, let's get on shall we?'

Chapter Two

With her old house, ten miles away, sold and having rented a small, modern, terraced house in the village of Wynenden, to be near to her new house, and to enable her to start integrating into village life. Katherine took the few days, before the work was due to start on Wynenden Farm, to continue to familiarise herself with the area on foot. Wynenden Village was not one she knew particularly well. Her work as an administrator at a Preparatory School, fifteen miles away, kept her busy during the week. Prior to her springtime walk, which had resulted in the discovery of Wynenden Farm, she had tended to visit villages around where her previous house was located, in the opposite direction to Wynenden.

She saw it as fate that she had been sent up to Wynenden School, an Independent Mixed School for children aged 3 to 18, to deliver some urgent paperwork and have a look around, because prior to a meeting the system at her school had crashed, and there was no chance of e-mailing the necessary paperwork to them. She was taken by the prettiness of the village, driving through that day. It had a main road running though it, this being the link between two main roads which both led down to the coast, but the heart of it was set just off this. The large village green, which played host to village events in the summer. A narrow lane looped round the green in an arch, which took you up first to the village primary school and a play area, and also playing fields, on the left hand side. Beyond them further up round the green, was the village hall followed by the Church. The remainder of the green, from the Church back down the other side of the arch, to the main road was filled with an eclectic mix of houses, built during different periods from Tudor to Victorian, all fairly substantial properties, and all originally owned as part of the Wynenden Park Estate, until death duties got in the way, and necessitated the sale of assets from time to time, to assist with the payment of these duties.

Opposite the green, along the far side of the main road was the public house – The Speckled Goose - a post office cum stores, a small Michelin Star Restaurant, a butchers, a terrace of Edwardian houses, a doctors surgery, a veterinary surgery and a garage, which was purely there for mechanical purposes rather than for the sale of new, or second-hand cars or fuel. Whilst the main road took away some of the rural character of the village, it ensured that there was enough passing trade to boost the resident businesses, and ensure their continued place within the village - a rare occurrence - with so many villages now without shops, pubs or any such kind of local business.

Further up the road from the public house, in the opposite direction to the shops, was a housing estate built in the 1970's. Perhaps innovative in their time, but now very dated, and rather an eyesore, in an otherwise picturesque village. But this was where Katherine had managed to rent her temporary house, so she couldn't complain too much.

Katherine had deliberately organised for completion on the houses, and the building works to start, during the time she had off for the two week October half term. Ignoring the piles of boxes, which ought to be unpacked, Katherine shrugged on her pink gilet, zipped some cash into her inside pocket, grabbed her keys and phone, and set off for a walk around the village.

Coming out of the housing estate, she turned right and walked along the pavement to the post office and stores and entered.

'Good Morning,' came a cheerful voice from behind the stores counter.

'Oh. Hello.'

'Nice Morning out there, lovely and crisp.'

'Mmm, yes, it is.' Katherine looked round for the newspapers, and spied them over by the window, pondering whether to go for intelligence and get something like The Times, or get something less highbrow. In the end she opted for The Times, and perused the magazines impressed by the range available, she picked up a copy of Hello! Magazine for some light reading, and took them to the till. 'Are you open on a Sunday?' she asked.

The older woman, with tightly permed, grey hair, who, Katherine estimated, was in her early sixties, clicked her tongue in disapproval, making Katherine feel as though she had committed a major faux pas. 'I'm afraid we are. I don't believe in it myself, but it's not me who owns this place. But I told them right from the start that I wasn't going to work on a Sunday. It's a day of rest and I'm in Church every Sunday morning.'

'Oh, OK. I just wanted to know if I'd be able to get a Sunday paper here?' She placed her paper and magazine on the counter.

The woman's eyes lit up. 'New to the village are you?' Katherine nodded. 'Which house have you moved to?'

Well, they're not backwards in coming forwards round here, thought Katherine, mildly irritated, and not wanting to proffer the information. 'It's just on the outskirts of the village.' She replied, hoping her vagueness would be enough. She ought to have known better.

'Really? Which one? Do you mean on the estate?' The woman's brow wrinkled in thought.

'Um, well I'm living there at the moment.' Perhaps ambiguity would halt the questions.

'At the moment, does that mean temporarily?'

I'll give her that, she's sharp thought Katherine. 'Er, yes. Just while I have work done on the house I've bought.'

'You must be Kitty!' exclaimed the woman. 'You've just bought Wynenden Farm haven't you? I'm Betty by the way.' She offered her hand, along with a beaming smile.

How on earth does she know who I am? Let alone which house I've bought? Privacy was the one thing which Katherine treasured the most. She liked to keep things to herself, having seen the way that gossip can be produced out of thin air, by parents at the Prep School, and experience from living in her previous village. Gingerly she took the woman's hand, and shook it.

'We've all been expecting you. You've caused great excitement in the village! Sir Geoffrey is very territorial about his Estate. We couldn't believe it when we heard that he had sold off Wynenden Farm! We'd never have believed it! Of course, that Andy Battle has been trying to get his hands on it for years, and Sir Geoffrey has refused to sell it to him. Some even said that he offered Sir Geoffrey two million pounds!' Betty paused for breath.

Katherine was startled by this news. No wonder Andrew - or Andy as he seemed to be known - was so furious that she had bought the house. But why on earth could he be so desperate to buy it? Granted, it was a lovely house, in a stunning position, with loads of potential, but even done up it probably wouldn't be worth half of what he had offered for it. And why had Sir Geoffrey sold it to her at below market price? When she had approached him, or rather his Estate Manager, Ted, about possibly purchasing the house, a price had been offered to her. She knew from having researched the local property market, that it was below market value, and despite her raising this point, -which some thought she was mad to do but her conscience told her to - with Ted, the price was not adjusted. Most would think her a fool for even suggesting that the price was too low, but she was honest, and she wanted to buy the house at a fair price. Properties like Wynenden Farm were like gold dust, most having already been snatched up, done up, and sold on at a huge profit.

'So, how did you manage to get Sir Geoffrey to sell you the house? We've all been speculating.' She looked eagerly at Katherine, not able to believe her luck at being one of the first to set eyes on her.

There's no way I'm giving her any information, thought Katherine. 'You appear to know a lot about me. How is that so?' She tried not to sound terse, but felt ridiculously violated.

'Oh, Dougie was overheard in the pub talking to one of his builders about the job, and Hetty who works there is such a gossip, she told anyone who would listen.'

Not the only one who likes to gossip, thought Katherine whilst making a mental note to ask Dougie not to discuss the house, or her, anywhere in public. She absolutely did not want her day to day life broadcast across the village. 'It seems that you are very well informed. I don't think I can really add to what you know.' And there's no way I'm answering your last question, she thought. She offered the money for the paper and magazine to Betty, and smiled as sweetly as she could, realising - perhaps a little late - that if she were grumpy, it would be all round the village in a flash, but the "grumpy" would evolve into "stuck up", "arrogant" or worse.

Sensing defeat, Betty took the money, and proffered the change, disappointed that she had not found out more, but still quietly delighted, that she had been the first to encounter the most talked about woman in the village. 'Lovely to meet you Kitty. Anything you want to know about the village, just pop in and ask. I'm always willing to help.'

'Thank you Betty, I will remember that.' And with a smile still fixed on her face, Katherine strolled to the door, doing her best not to bolt for it and run. Just as she pulled the door closed behind her, she heard Betty dialling a number, and start gossiping to someone about her down the telephone. She rolled her eyes, and sighed, hoping that tomorrow, she would be old news. She continued up the road, pausing to read the simple menu at the village's Michelin Star pride and joy – The Restaurant at Wynenden – it sounded delectable, seasonal, not overly fussy, and relatively reasonably priced. Perhaps she should have a cele-bratory meal there with some friends? She pondered. Her pondering's took her on to Wynenden Butchers where, bracing herself for another interrogation, she joined the queue in the tiny shop. Murmurs of "Good Morning" were made and to avoid any further interaction, Katherine stu-diously studied the interesting array of products available in the chilled display unit, until it was her turn.

She smiled at the short, rotund, bald figure, behind the counter. 'Please could I have a couple of the lamb chops, and a couple of the lamb, mint and apple sausages?'

'Of course.' He silently went about his work. 'That'll be £6.70 thank you.' He smiled at her.

'Thanks,' she replied, handing over £20, relieved that the butcher was not as inquisitive as Betty.

'Don't look so worried,' he chortled, handing her the change, 'we're not all as forward as Betty.'

Katherine felt her body relax, unaware that she had been holding her breath. She smiled, and said diplomatically 'Well, she appears to be very friendly.' Suspecting that it was the butcher, Betty had phoned when she had left the shop.

'Aye, that she is. She means well, and she's got a heart of gold, but working in that shop doesn't really get her out into the real world, if you know what I mean. Most people don't want to chat for hours these days, they just want to rush in and straight out again. I think she gets a bit lonely in there sometimes. A bit starved of real conversation. Anyway, I'm Bob, Bob Bond, pleased to meet you Kitty.' He offered a clean hand, which had just been washed under steaming hot water.

'Pleased to meet you too Bob.' She responded, taking his hand, and thinking that she would forever be known as Kitty in the village, and not Katherine. Was there any point in correcting them?

'Welcome to the village. You'll get used to us!' He was interrupted by the tinkle of the bell over the door as it opened. 'Morning Mrs Bush.' He waved at the sparrow like figure hurrying into the shop.

'Bye,' called Katherine making a speedy exit, in case Mrs Bush turned out to be working undercover for Betty.

The remainder of her stroll was, fortunately, uneventful and upon returning home Katherine settled down with the house plans, the kitchen plans, and the piles of catalogues and samples she had gathered. Now the fun would really begin, as she buried herself excitedly in the many decisions which still had to be made.

Chapter Three

A couple of days later, Katherine was up early so that she could get to the farmhouse before the builders arrived for Day One, of the restoration. She pulled her eight year old, bright red, VW Golf into the drive, and parked it on some flattened rough grass. She got out, grabbed her trusty rucksack - which was packed with plans and a flask of coffee - from the back seat, locked up, and walked silently over the dew drenched drive. Barely recognizable as a drive, because it was so overgrown, the odd bald patch where gravel or some other kind of unrecognizable surface had been, indicated that it was not part of the garden.

She stopped, and drank in the glorious silence, the odd tweet from a bird awakening, and nothing else. From a distance, the house looked like it had some kind of fuzzy hairdo. A couple of windows peeped out from the mass of brambles and ivy, which covered the house from ground to roof. Again, she trod her way carefully to the front door, and opened up. Quietly she walked around, absorbing all the decay and neglect, drinking it in to store away as memories, so that she would remember how much the house had changed in years to come, feeling that photos alone would not do it justice. She shivered slightly, and momentarily felt an unsettling eeriness. She shook her head to clear it, and moved away into another room.

The silence was broken shortly afterwards by the distant rumble of vehicles, as they made their way cautiously up the narrow lane. It was as though someone had said "lights, camera, action!". In an instant, the drive was full of cars and vans, and there were two lorries piled high with scaffolding poles and other building equipment, queuing and blocking the narrow lane.

Katherine ran cautiously down the stairs and out through the front door. 'Morning Dougie!' she grinned.

'You ready for us?' he laughed.

'As I'll ever be! Bring it on!'

Men swarmed all over the site in purposeful mode. Several were set to clear the site immediately surrounding the house, to enable ease of access and the building of the small garden room extension, and to enable the scaffolding to go up securely. Katherine went over a couple of points with Dougie, and then retreated to her car. Taking out the flask off coffee and sipping the hot liquid, she wrinkled her nose up at the slightly plasticky taste, which was always the unfortunate consequence of drinking a hot liquid out of plastic - particularly a flask lid - and wished she'd brought a china mug to drink from. She made a mental note to do so next time.

As far as she was concerned, watching the workmen working, and her house begin to emerge from its Sleeping Beautyesque slumber, was more exciting than going to the cinema. It was incredible how much had been cleared by the time they stopped two hours later, for a coffee break. There were beeping of horns in the lane as another lorry, delivering a portaloo for the workmen, tried to get the scaffolding lorries to move. With a bit of negotiation, the builders carried the portaloo off the lorry themselves, and let the driver have the fun task of reversing back up the single track lane. With the drive blocked there was nowhere for him to turn.

Unable to get her car out, and with no desire to get in the way of the workmen, Katherine took a stroll up the lane to stretch her legs and warm up, as the chill in the air had settled on her whilst sitting for so long in the car without her engine running. Upon her return she gasped at the sight of her house, now externally free from its fuzzy hair.

'Looks a bit different, doesn't it?' grinned Dougie.

'You can say that again! It looks huge! So much bigger than I thought it would be, it's amazing!'

'It certainly is a lovely example of a Tudor house. Once we get the ivy off the inside, you will be able to see so many more beams. There are some pretty chunky ones there.'

'Great! I can't wait.' She studied the building. 'I never knew there were two fireplaces. How come I missed them? There's a chimney at that end, as well as the large one in the centre. Where's the other fireplace?'

'Bricked up I suppose, we can have a look when we've cleared the ivy off. Maybe it's just covered in that pesky stuff?' He looked thoughtful.

'OK. So when's the scaffolding going up?'

'As soon as. I would hope they'll make a start by mid afternoon. They'll keep going as long as it's light, but it should all be up by the end of tomorrow.'

'And it's definitely being covered?'

'Oh yes, don't you worry. That house will be more water tight than it has been in years.'

It had, perhaps, been a little extravagant of Katherine to insist on the scaffolding being covered in thick plastic, to protect the house from rain. But she didn't want anything to slow the build down. With winter approaching, she didn't want to get caught out and for the house to end up filled with rain or snow, because the roof was off. It was hoped that the majority of the roof timbers were going to stay, but if more needed to be replaced it would delay the re-roofing, which in turn would have a knock on effect to the rest of the build. And it would be typical that the bright, sunny, autumnal days would instantly change into wet, hideous, weather.

Satisfied that there were going to be no further dramatic changes to the house that day, Katherine negotiated her car out into the lane, and drove home to spend more time poring over the brochures, narrowing down the choice of fixtures and fittings, the radiators and the million and one other things she needed to make decisions on, so that products could be ordered and not delay the works.

By the end of the week the scaffolding was up, the brambles and ivy had been ripped away - both internally and externally - and work was starting on stripping the roof and the internal walls - those with Listed Building Consent to remove - were starting to come down. The builders bucked the trend and turned up prior to their 8 a.m. start time, worked hard, took the same breaks at the same time each day, and finished at 4 p.m.

Katherine lay in bed and stretched, it was Friday morning and she was aware that next week she would be back at work, and unable to be on site every day. Fortunately, she had managed to persuade the school to let her start an hour earlier each day for the next few months, and have Wednesday afternoon off for the remainder of the Michaelmas Term and also the Lent Term. Though not ideal, this at least ensured that she would be on site once a week, and if anything urgent cropped up she'd just have to deal with it. When the evenings became lighter, she would be able to go to the house after work each day, until then, she would have to make do.

As she dressed and breakfasted, she thought smugly that the weasel-faced, rat of an ex-husband of hers, was missing out big time. Married for twenty years, relatively blissfully she had thought, she and Rex had been desperate for a family from day one of getting married when she was twenty-three. Sadly, despite operation after operation, and treatment after treatment, nothing happened until, suddenly, at the age of forty-three she became pregnant. Assuming that it was an early start to the menopause, she had gone to her G.P. only to discover that she was pregnant. They had, she thought, been thrilled at the prospect of finally fulfilling their dream of parenthood, after such a struggle. Rex had become more attentive than he had for a long time; they excitedly read the books, the magazines, surfed the net, and drenched themselves in the forthcoming joy. Tragically, at sixteen weeks, and totally out of the blue, Katherine miscarried. She was devastated at having come so close to such joy, and having it so cruelly snatched away. She thought that Rex felt the same, but just when she felt nothing worse could possibly happen, and in the depths of deep despair, he left her.

Still numb from the shock of losing the baby, his callousness was uncomprehending to her. Blocking it out for several weeks, hoping he was going to walk back through the door as though nothing had happened. When the reality finally hit that he wasn't going to, it was the last straw and pushed her into a deep depression which was, over time, overcome with the help of medication, counselling and the support, care, consideration, love and kindness of her closest friends and her parents. In the cold light of day she had wondered, and still wondered, whether she ever knew him. How could someone who was supposed to be your life partner treat you like that? How on earth could there have been, in her view, no indication that something was wrong in their marriage? In time she came to believe that he was having a midlife crisis. He'd left her a week after her miscarriage, for a much younger woman. He never told her, and she never wanted to know, how long it had been going on, because that would mean that the special few weeks she had experienced of being pregnant would be devalued and, worse, the thought that maybe he had not even wanted their precious baby.

Now, four years later, he was forty-eight and had had a string of girlfriends, each younger than the last, and in amongst these he had tried to come back to Katherine. He begged, pleaded, promised, but she could no longer trust him and no longer loved him. She felt that she would just be a stop gap until some flighty young thing came along and took his fancy. Realizing he had burnt his bridges, he'd tried to get more than his fair share of their marital home, but by then Katherine was stronger and the fight kicked in. Why should she move? Why should he get more than he deserved after the way he had treated her? There were times when she felt he didn't deserve a penny. Yes, they may have made money on their house, but why should he get any of it? Fortunately the Judge presiding over the case was fair and split everything equally, and also ruled that Katherine should have the option to stay in the house. She re-mortgaged, gave her ex his share of the profit, and washed her hands of him. The struggle to pay the large mortgage each month was worth being free of him. From time to time she saw him, strutting around, dressing too young for is age, acting eighteen not forty-eight, and she felt sorry for him. He was all about appearance now, and she'd heard on the grapevine that he'd blown his share of the house on a flash car and splurging on girlfriends, and now lived in a pokey one bedroom rented flat in a less than desirable area.

But, here she was now, having moved on and glad that she was no longer with him, but mourned the loss of a close relationship, someone to talk to, to share experiences with, someone to comfort her in a way that best friends couldn't when both her parents had died in a car crash eighteen months ago. As their only child she had inherited their mortgage free house, savings, pensions and other assets. Leaving her, after inheritance tax, with a considerable lump sum, enabling her to buy Wynenden Farmhouse outright, pay for the renovation and, combined with her profit from her marital home, a nest egg for her future. Pushing these now melancholy thoughts away, she made herself reflect on how lucky she was, packed her rucksack for the day and set off to the farmhouse.

'Morning.' She smiled cheerfully to the builders as they all started for the day.

'Do you want to have a look at this fireplace then?' asked Dougie.

'Great! You've cleared the ivy then?' He nodded. 'Is it an open fireplace?'

'Not at the moment, it looks like it has been bricked up at some point. We'll have to pull some bricks away to see what's behind.'

'You sure that's ok? Do we need permission or anything?' Katherine had played it very much above board. Sir Geoffrey had been happy for her to have meetings with the local Conservation Officer, Planning Officer and Architect to discuss what may, or may not be, carried out and make the relevant applications, before exchange and completion as the house was Grade II Listed and the primary concern was to protect the house from inappropriate work or changes, and preserve its character and history.

'I had a word with the Conservation chap yesterday and he's happy for us to investigate, he'll probably pop out sometime today to see what we're up to anyway.'

'OK, that's fine then. Let's go. It'd be so exciting if there's another inglenook fireplace there!'

She and Dougie watched as Pete, one of Dougie's workers, started carefully tapping away at a brick. After a while they turned away and poured over plans whilst the banging and crashing echoed through the house all around them and the more refined tap, tap, tapping from Pete carried on.

'Bloody Hell!' shouted Pete, jumping back.

Katherine and Dougie started in surprise. 'What's up?' asked Dougie.

Pete's normally tanned and rosy face, had gone a peculiar shade of white. He pointed at the small opening he had made, about six bricks square.

Dougie strode over and peered into the dark recess. 'Shit!' he swore, leaping back. 'Sorry Katherine.'

Puzzled, Katherine couldn't work out what would freak two grown men out. 'What is it? Let me have a look.' She moved forward.

'I don't think you should,' said Dougie.

'Why ever not? It can't be that bad?' She looked from one to the other.

They glanced at one another, then Dougie spoke. 'There's ... There's a skeleton in there.'

'You're joking?' She paused, 'you *are* joking aren't you?' She looked nervously at them, and realized that they weren't. Her stomach bottomed out, and she felt a wave of nausea.

Chapter Four

A swarm of police vehicles arrived a while later. After calling the police, Katherine and the builders left the building and stayed in their vehicles to await further instructions, nothing was to be disturbed. Katherine sat alone in her car shaking, clutching her coffee to her in an attempt to calm and warm her. Surely it must be a joke or something? It had been the grim realization that, apart from being virtually impossible, no one in their right mind would have bricked themselves up into a fireplace and, if they hadn't, then someone else had, and in that case the person must have been dead before they were bricked in. In other words it must have been murder. She trembled at the thought, the thought that something so awful had happened to someone, but not just that, that it had happened in her house, her dream house. She rested her cold, clammy, head on the steering wheel. A knock on the window made her start. She looked up to see a tall man using his fingers to indicate for her to put her window down. She fumbled with the keys and pressed the down button.

'Mrs Muier?' he asked.

'Yes.'

'I'm Detective Inspector Allix. I'd like to ask you a couple of questions if that's alright?' He looked questioningly at her. His face was kind but serious, with crinkles around his eyes from days off from his job when he could relax and smile. Katherine noticed a tiny scar on his chin, a result of his occupation or some other accident she wondered? She got out of the car and realized then how tall he was, at least 6' 2" she thought.

'I'm not sure that I can help you really,' she replied.

'Perhaps you could just tell me in your own words what happened this morning?' He looked kindly at her.

She did her best to recount what had happened, all the while D.I. Allix listened patiently, whilst slightly off to one side a non-uniformed woman made notes.

'And how long have you owned the house?'

'I completed last week. Tell me, what happened to whoever it was? Why are they there?'

'I don't really know any more than you have told me at the moment Mrs Muier. It will be sometime until I do. I'm afraid I'm going to have to ask you and your builders to leave the site.'

'How long for? They've only just started!'

'I'm not sure. Forensics will be here for some time. We are treating this as a suspicious death, and until such a time as we know more, and are satisfied that we have obtained all the evidence we require from this site, it will remain cordoned off. I'm sorry.'

Katherine felt irrationally ambivalent. On the one hand she was horrified that someone had seemingly come to an unpleasant end, but on the other hand she was desperate for the work to carry on at the house, and was irritated that they had to stop for an unknown period of time. The momentum which had begun was halted, and she worried that it may never get back to the way that it had been. She was aware of the D.I. talking, and shook her head to clear it. 'Sorry, what did you say? I guess I'm a bit shaken up.'

'That's understandable. I was just saying if you could give your details to my colleague, Detective Sergeant Windsor.' He indicated to the woman standing near him who had been taking notes. 'So that we can contact you when necessary, then you can go home. Would you like someone to accompany you?'

'No, no that's fine, thanks. I'll just speak to Dougie, my builder' She pointed to him, it looked like his details were already being taken.

'Fine. Thank you for your cooperation. We'll be in touch.' Katherine watched his tall, suited, figure stride off towards her house and speak to the uniformed policeman who was standing guard outside the front door. A few words and a nod and he disappeared inside.

There was a knock on the door, making Katherine start. She'd been curled up on the sofa with a cup of tea, brooding over the events of the day. Stiffly, she uncurled, feeling every one of her forty-seven years and more, and padded to the door. Cautiously she peered round it. It was Dougie. She smiled at the familiar face.

'Hi, come in. I was just having a cuppa, fancy one?' She led him through to the small, insipid, kitchen and flicked the switch on the kettle.

'I just thought I'd pop in to see how you are? You know, after this morning?' His worried face searched hers for an indication of how she was bearing up.

'Oh, I'm fine,' she sighed. 'I'll be back to myself by tomorrow. It's my own stupid fault. I shouldn't have taken a look. You know the saying "curiosity killed the cat" well I should have known better. I can't get rid of the image of that hideous grimace on the skull. Maybe they all look gruesome and I'm letting my imagination run away with me, but it really looked as though - whoever it was - was screaming, and doing so right up until the moment of death.' She shivered again at the memory.

'I know what you mean,' replied Dougie, 'best not to dwell on it.'

'Do you think it had been there for a while? I mean, do you think it could be really old, like hundreds of years?' she looked hopefully at him.

'Hmm, not sure, unlikely though. The fireplace would have been in use for many, many years. I can't believe it would have been bricked up for that long.'

'What about the bricks? Surely you could tell? I mean, if they are old, then the skeleton would be old?'

'Not necessarily. Reclaimed bricks could have been used. Doesn't necessarily mean anything.'

'So, what happens now?'

Dougie looked glum. This was the perfect job to keep them going through the winter. The last thing he wanted was a delay, which would mean a delay in payments be-cause the work was behind, and he had no other job lined up for his team until the spring, having put all his eggs in one basket. 'We have no choice. We have to wait until they have finished investigating the site, but I can't see us being back there on Monday.' He followed her with his mug of tea into the sitting room, and lowered his plump frame into a squashy chair.

'It'd be nice to know what was going on. They said they'd let me know. I guess they'll have police outside the house twenty-four hours a day until they have finished, won't they?'

'I would have thought so, but not got a clue really. Once word gets out they'll be a handful of ghoulish people who'll want to poke around.'

'Damn! That's the last thing I want, people poking around. I was hoping the work could carry on in quiet oblivion, the more people who know about this, the more they'll be nosing around. And what about the security risk once the police have gone? Do you think there'll be people snooping about on site after dark? What about the materials? There'll be a higher risk of them getting stolen, particularly those old, reclaimed, Kent Peg Tiles.'

'I know, they're twice the price of new ones. I suppose I'll have to get some kind of security up there initially. Just until the fuss has died down.'

'Oh, great, more cost. Sorry Dougie, I didn't mean it like that, I'm just hacked off that something I was so excited about has come crashing down, and to add insult to injury, it's going to cost me more.'

'That's ok Kitty. I'm as annoyed as you are. Still, I can't sit around here all afternoon, I'd best get back and do some paperwork whilst I have the time. Thanks for the tea.'

'No problem. If I hear anything, I'll let you know, but perhaps we can keep a lid on this as much as possible?' she looked at him questioningly.

'My lips are sealed. Though I think once it's got out, it'll be hard to stop the floodgate of rumours.'

Katherine sighed again, let him out, and went back to brooding on the sofa with her, now cold, cup of tea. Barely had she had a good wallow in her misery, when there was another knock at the door. This time it was D.I. Allix, accompanied by D.S. Windsor. Her offer of tea was refused, and she ushered them into the sitting room.

D.I. Allix waited until Katherine had settled herself, before he spoke. 'How are you?' he enquired.

'Oh, fine, you know, bit spooked, but ok thanks.' She glanced at D.S. Windsor who was sitting there poised, ready, and alert, in a black trouser suit and cream blouse buttoned to a respectfully high level, and low-healed, black lace up, shoes. Dull but practical. Her hair was a sort of mid-brown-cum-mousy mix, of collar length, tucked firmly behind her ears, making her look slightly fierce. Katherine glanced back to D.I. Allix, who looked a lot less fierce than his colleague.

'The skeleton has been removed now, but we will of course need access to the house for a while longer. Please be assured that we will hand it back to you as soon as it is possible.'

'Thanks. Can you tell me anything more about the ..., well...?' Her voice trailed off, and she shrugged and fiddled with her hands, not willing to say the "skeleton" word.

'Not a great deal at this moment, but I have been told that the skeleton is female, and younger, rather than older. Obviously, when I have further information, I, or one of my colleagues, will update you.'

He rose to go. Katherine got up to show them out, then made herself a replacement cup of hot tea, flopped down on the sofa again, and flicked the television on to watch the local news. She'd just missed the headlines, and the presenters went straight into their lead story, the discovery of remains at a house in Wynenden. Oh no! thought Katherine. The whole world is going to know now! It felt like the situation was a train careering out of control, and there was nothing she could do to stop it. She felt any chance of peacefully doing up her house, was now blown out of the water. Everyone in the village is going to be trying to track me down to get the latest, I'll never have any peace, she thought agitatedly. Barely had the story finished, when the phone started ringing. She hesitated, wondering whether she ought to answer it. But what if it's a friend who knows nothing about it? Cautiously, she picked up the phone and said hesitantly 'hello?'

'Kitty?'

She relaxed, it was Libby, her best friend. 'Libs, how are you?' she replied, delighted to hear a friendly voice, 'I was going to call you later.'

'I've saved you the trouble. What's up? You sounded rather guarded when you answered the phone?'

'You can say that again! You are never going to believe what happened today…!' She proceeded to tell her best friend in great detail, the events of the day. '… so you see I wasn't quite sure who was going to be on the other end, when I picked up the phone!' she finished.

'Honestly! I can't leave you alone for a minute without you causing trouble!' she laughed. 'Want me to come over? I can ditch dinner with James and be over for 8 o'clock.'

'Thanks, but I'll be fine, and there's no way I'm going to be responsible for you and James missing out on your date night. I don't think James would ever forgive me! Really, I'm fine, I'll catch up with you soon.'

'That's what I was phoning for, to get a date out of you. When are you free?'

'How about next Wednesday afternoon? I can't see the builders being allowed back on site by then, why don't you come and have a sarni with me here. Say about 1.30?'

'Great! I'll see you then.'

'Have a nice evening!'

'Don't worry, I will! Bye.'

Katherine smiled to herself, she could always rely on her best mate to perk her up. The phone rang again. 'OK, so what did you forget?' she laughed.

'Oh, er…,' said a male voice.

'Oh! Sorry, I thought you were someone else.' She paused. She recognized the voice, but her brain was grappling to identify the name.

'Oh, right,' came the voice. 'Katherine?'

'Yes?'

'It's Ted. Ted Armstrong.'

'Hi Ted. How are you?' Ted, being Sir Geoffrey's Estate Manager.

'I'm fine thanks. I've heard about what happened today at the farmhouse. Are you ok?' His voice was soft and gentle.

'I'm fine, thanks for asking. Bit of a shock that's for sure.' She liked Ted, he was always kind and courteous towards her and, she suspected, to everyone he dealt with. Some might class him as old fashioned in his manner, by the way he stood up when a woman entered the room, held the door open for them and was generally very polite. Pity more people weren't like that in this me, me, me, culture of today Katherine had often mused.

'Good. Um ...,' he hesitated again.

'Was there something else?'

'Sir Geoffrey has asked me, to ask you, what you know about the remains which were found? He thought you might know more than had been presented on the news.'

'No, I'm afraid I don't. There's very little to tell, and what there is to know, has already been on the news. We're not allowed near the house until the police tell us the builders can start again.'

He sighed. She had ascertained from her own encounters with Sir Geoffrey, that he was a man who always expected - and got - his own way, which made for uncomfortable situations at times with his staff, and guessed that Ted would be grilled again, and again, and demands as to why he didn't know more, would be repeated. 'Ok. Well if you do happen to hear any more, could you possibly give me a ring? I know Sir Geoffrey is keen to find out as much as possible.'

'Of course I will, no problem. Thanks for ringing.'

'Thanks,' he hesitated again and Katherine got the impression there was something else on his mind, 'bye then.' The phone clicked dead, and Katherine looked at it, puzzled.

Chapter Five

Katherine spent the weekend hidden away, only slipping out in her car, to avoid the curiosity of those in the village which, she was in no doubt, was reaching fever pitch. A little extreme perhaps, to get in her car to drive to another village to buy the weekend newspapers, when the shop was a few minutes walk away, and stocked the very papers she wanted. But she wasn't going to take the risk, and justified it by convincing herself that it was only for this weekend.

Monday came with the start of children freshly back from their two week break. Getting to work an hour earlier, and starting at 7.30 a.m. rather than 8.30 a.m, meant that Katherine was able to plough through a large pile of paperwork with no interruptions. Far more than she would normally be able to get through in a morning, simply because the phone wasn't ringing, and there wasn't constant interruptions as parents, prospective parents, children, teachers, delivery drivers and the like, flowed in and out of the office, in the normal wave of activities. 8.30 a.m. brought in the rest of the office staff. The prep school was large, with 700 pupils, but it was divided into three separate areas; kindergarten and pre-prep were in one building in an area of the school grounds, prep which was Years 3 to

6 were in another building also in a different area of the school grounds, and finally, the seniors in Years 7 and 8 -which took them to the age of 13 - was in yet another building, one which adjoined the administrative offices and Headmasters' office. They all shared the same facilities i.e. sports fields, music rooms, sports/assembly hall, refectory and all had plenty of opportunities to come together as one whole school.

All the office staff, including the Headmasters' Secretary/Personal Assistant, shared a large, open plan, office, off a welcoming entrance hall in the new wing of the school. It was light and airy and a pleasurable environment in which to work. In the entrance area were a couple of sofas and a coffee table, with a neat arrangement of school brochures and magazines for visitors to peruse, whilst waiting for their appointments. The walls were filled with photographs, paintings and works of art, created by the children. All ages from the school equally represented, a good advertisement for the school.

'Morning Katherine,' called Liz, coming through the entrance door and making a "would you like a cup of coffee sign" as she headed off to the small kitchen located off the left hand side of the entrance. Having made an affirmative sign, Katherine ploughed on until Liz placed a mug of freshly brewed coffee on her desk. She'd been followed in by Jane and Mary, who was the Heads' secretary.

'Well?' asked Liz expectantly. Her eyes sparkling through her round, gold-rimmed, spectacles.

'Well what?' smiled Katherine back, knowing fully what Liz meant.

'The house on the news? It is yours isn't it? It's got to be. How many houses can there be in Wynenden, that are complete wrecks and where building work has just started?'

'OK, you've got me there! But just keep it to yourselves, I don't want to be the main topic of gossip for the school. I think I've got enough of that in the village.'

'Goes without saying,' she replied. Jane and Mary who were listening, whilst taking off their coats and setting up for the day, nodded too.

'Well, there's not a lot to tell, other than what was on the news. I've not been told any more by the police, and we're not allowed at the house until they've finished with it, and I've no idea how long that will be.'

'What a pain! The builders have only just started,' remarked Jane. 'But were you there when they found it? Did you see it? What was it like?'

'Don't be such a ghoul Jane!' reprimanded Mary.

'Oh, come on! You can't say you're not interested?' she retorted.

'Interested, but I don't need the gory details!'

'Yes, I was there, and yes I did see it. But no, I don't have a clue about anything else, how's that?' She was silenced by the school bell ringing outside the office, calling the children to assembly. 'Anyway, if I have any more to tell, I will tell you. Don't worry!' With that, they all settled down to the hustle and bustle of the days' work.

Monday evening came and went. Tuesday past by and Katherine was wondering if she would ever hear from the police. Surely it couldn't take them that long to search the house? She'd just finished washing up her supper dishes when there was a knock at the door. Katherine frowned. She wasn't expecting anyone. She put the chain on the front door and opened it. It was D.I. Allix. 'Hold on a moment.' She indicated to the chain, closed the door, slid the chain back and opened the door fully. He was accompanied again by D.I. Windsor.

'Could we come in please Mrs Muier?' he asked politely.

'Please.' She indicated the way through to the sitting room and offered them tea, which was again turned down. Sitting in identical places to their previous visit, Katherine got a sense of déjà vu. She noticed that he looked a little more tired and drawn than his last visit, like he'd not slept for the past four nights. However D.S. Windsor looked as fresh as a daisy, as though nothing ever got to her, it was just a job, and it all washed off the hard exterior.

He cleared his throat. 'I wanted to keep you in the picture Mrs Muier,'

'Does that mean we can start building works again?' she interrupted.

'No. I'm afraid not. We need a little longer. I have more information I can give you about whose remains were discovered, dental records were checked and her parents have been informed.' She looked questioningly at him. 'I'm afraid it was a local girl who went missing ten years ago. Her name was Cecilia Stillingfleet. She was sixteen when she went missing, which we believe was when she was killed. There is no doubt that she was murdered.'

Katherine felt the bile rising in her throat and let out a sob. 'Poor girl. But who would have done such a thing? I mean, a young girl. Why?'

'That's what we have got to find out. Did you know the girl? Know anything about her?'

She shook her head. 'No, I didn't, sorry. I only moved here a couple of weeks ago, before that I lived about fifteen miles away. I don't really know anything about the village, or the people in it, though I vaguely remember hearing about her going missing from the news back then.'

'That's OK, I needed to ask.'

'If she was local, do you mean she lived in this village?'

'Yes, and her parents still do.'

'Oh no! The poor things! They must be beside themselves.'

'They are very distraught, naturally, but they have had ten years of not knowing whether their daughter was dead or alive. Whilst they have always clung onto the hope that she was alive, they do at least now know, which is small consolation. Every time there was the hint of a sighting, or potential new evidence as to her whereabouts, their hopes were raised.'

They sat in silence for a few moments. 'I guess, if she was a local girl, then a lot of people in the village knew her?'

'Yes. When she went missing, the whole village pulled together in an effort to find her. As time has gone by people have apparently come to their own conclusions about whether she was dead or alive, but nothing really prepares one for the stark reality of death.'

He looked sad, she thought, surprised that he would feel anything for someone he did not know. Another body. Another day. It must be part of his regular routine.

'Anyway, if you hear of anything that may be of help to us, please call on the numbers I gave you. Anything, no matter how insignificant.' He rose to go.

'Of course. Anything I can do to help, I will.'

'Thanks. We'll be in touch. Goodnight.'

'Night,' she replied absent mindedly as she closed the door behind them. Not a great drinker, she did, however, feel in need of something to fortify her and rummaged through some boxes in the hall until she found the bottle of brandy she used to "feed" her Christmas cake each year, and poured a generous glug into a tumbler from the kitchen.

She sank down into the sofa and clutched the brandy to her, sipping it from time to time, feeling the liquid burn its way down into her stomach, warming her from the inside, but not enough to take away the shaking that had started and the clamminess of her hands as the reality set in. A young girl, barely a woman, murdered and bricked up in her house. The hideousness of it was hard to comprehend. How could a person take another's life? And how evil must you be to go that step further and take a young person, or child's, life? She reached for the phone and dialled Libby.

After an agonizing few rings Libby answered. 'Hello?'

'Libs, it's me,' she sniffed.

'Kitty, what's wrong? You sound dreadful,' said Libby slightly alarmed.

'The police have just been, they know who the, who the ...' she couldn't say it. She paused to compose herself. 'It was a girl. A local girl. She was only sixteen, Libs. Sixteen and somebody snatched her life away. How could they do that?'

'Oh, Kitty. How awful. Poor child. Do the police know any more? Have a motive?'

'No. Apparently she's been missing for ten years, they think she died then. She lived in the village, her parents

43

still live here. Apparently they kept hoping she was alive and would turn up one day.'

'How terrible for them, utterly ghastly.' Libby closed her eyes as she pushed away the nightmare thoughts of how she would feel if one of her two darling children disappeared, to have that daily struggle, not knowing, imagining what horrific things could be happening to them. The agony of not being able to help or to protect. 'Shall I come round? James is not back yet, but I could get my neighbour to pop in, to look after the children, until he does.'

'No, I'll be fine Libby. Really, it's just the shock and it's not even my own child. I can't imagine how completely devastated, and bereft, her parents must be feeling. Really, I'll be fine.' She continued as Libby protested. 'I just needed to hear a friendly voice, to tell someone. But please, don't say anything to anyone. I don't know who else knows.'

'Of course I won't Kitty. Call me anytime if you need me, and I do mean anytime. I'll see you tomorrow for lunch anyway. Go and have a hot bath and curl up, try to get some sleep.'

'I think I will. See you tomorrow. Bye.' She'd momentarily forgotten that she was seeing her friend the next day and, comforted by that thought, and having just spoken to her, she slowly sipped the remainder of her brandy, calming herself down. She closed her eyes for a few moments and opened them suddenly, having remembered that she'd promised to phone Ted if there were any developments. Should I? But if I don't and it's on the news, I'll have let him down, she mused. Reluctantly, she decided she ought to tell him. After all, it had happened whilst Sir Geoffrey still owned the house, and she vaguely thought that Ted had told her he had worked at the Estate for ten, or eleven years, so maybe he and Sir Geoffrey could help the police?

She found his number in her phone and dialled it.

'Hello?'

'Ted? It's Katherine.'

'Katherine. Hi, how are you?' His voice change from businesslike, to soft, when he realized who it was.

'I'm fine thanks,' she replied automatically. 'You asked me to keep you updated about what was happening at the farmhouse.'

'Yes. Any news?'

'The police have been this evening. The remains were of a girl, a local girl, Cecilia Stillingfleet. Apparently she went missing about ten years ago.'

'No! Really? Gosh, that's awful. I remember the up-roar when she went missing. To start with nobody believed her parents. She was a bit of a wild thing, by all accounts, but once the village realized it was serious, and the police were involved, everyone turned out to help. Searching the village, the Estate, everywhere they could think of. It was shortly after I arrived here, not a very pleasant thing to happen, and in an unspoken kind of way, it has always hung over the village.'

'I thought you should know, but I don't know how many others do. Her parents know, but it might be an idea to keep this to yourself. Though I guess you will have to tell Sir Geoffrey?'

'He and Lady Susan ought to be told. Particularly as it occurred at one of their properties. This is dreadful. I suppose I ought to go and tell them now.'

'I would imagine the police are going to want to speak to them, and you and anyone else who works, or worked, on the Estate at that time. Sorry to be the bearer of such grim news.'

'Please don't worry. Thank you for telling me. I'd best get off and break the news to them. Thanks. Bye.'

Katherine decided she'd had enough of the day and ran herself a long, hot, bath, adding some comforting lavender bath oil to sooth her. After half an hour she was visibly relaxing, and took herself off to bed to read for a while to wind down. Reaching for the bedside lamp to switch it off, having calmed and settled herself, she jumped in alarm as the phone rang. Who on earth is phoning at this time of night? It was 11 p.m.

'Hello?' she answered cautiously.

'Katherine, I'm so sorry to disturb you.' It was Ted. 'But Sir Geoffrey is absolutely insistent that I phone you, he needs to see you.'

'What? Now?!'

'He wanted to, but I've calmed him down and persuaded him that it's not a good idea, that a few hours won't make a difference.' He sounded incredibly apologetic and had hated having to phone her at that time of night, but when his boss became insistent about something, there was no other choice. 'Could you come up to the house tomorrow morning?'

'No. Sorry, I'm working and there is no way I can get out of it,' she said firmly. 'I could be up there for three o'clock,' she conceded reluctantly.

'Is that the earliest? Are you sure?' Sir Geoffrey was not going to be happy about it.

'I'm afraid so. Tell him I will be there at 3 o'clock. Now, I have work tomorrow and I need my sleep, good night.' She put the receiver down feeling decidedly grumpy and wide awake, which made her feel even grumpier.

Ted looked at his phone, his heart sinking. Not only had he managed to upset Katherine, but he knew it was going to take all his tact and diplomacy to restrain Sir Geoffrey from going round to see her in the middle of the night, to demand information.

By 1 a.m. Katherine was still awake. The more she stayed awake, the more agitated she became, which made her more awake. It was a vicious circle. She reluctantly got up and made herself a cup of camomile tea, and took it to bed to sip and read her book, making a concerted effort to push away her anger and focus on the book. At 2 a.m. she switched the light off, snuggled down and hoped for the best. She did drift off, but it was an uncomfortable, nightmare-ridden sleep, tossing and turning. She awoke exhausted, and not in the least prepared for a morning at the office. At least, she thought, there was the blessing that it was just the morning she had to get through, and not a whole day.

Chapter Six

The morning had had to be caffeine filled to keep her alert and on top of her job and, having had a light lunch and a good chat with Libby, Katherine just wanted to curl up and go to sleep on the sofa. Instead, she found herself driving up to the stunning stone mansion, which was Wynenden Park, set in 2000 acres of rolling countryside and farmland. Normally a drive up to the "big house" as it was known in the village, filled her with excitement. As an enthusiastic member of the National Trust, she adored looking round large country piles, absorbing the history, and imagining what life must have been like in years gone by. But this afternoon she felt tired and lethargic, and not in the best of moods to face the grilling she was expecting from Sir Geoffrey. Her few dealings with him had been pleasant. He had always been respectful and a perfect gentleman, not living up to the reputation he seemed to have as a tyrant. But if what Ted had said last night was true, and he was on a mission to grill her, then their encounter may not be so civil.

She pulled up to a halt in front of the imposing stone steps, and looked at the forlorn façade. It was a house which had seen better days, days when money was no object and staff were abundant. Unfortunately, dwindling fortunes had resulted in the house gradually falling into a decline, with only the bare minimum of maintenance being able to be funded. It was a sad state of affairs, but not one that was unusual in this day and age. She got out of the car into the fine, misting, drizzle, which had started, and reluctantly walked up the steps, ringing the push bell to the right of the door. She thought she heard it vaguely ring in the distance, but wasn't sure. After what seemed like a lifetime she eventually heard a posse of dogs barking and yapping, and a motley crew of ageing Labradors, terriers and several unidentified mixes, bounced towards the half glass door to greet her. Following in their wake was Ted, his face alight with a smile when he saw her.

'Hi, come in. Sorry it took so long, we were right at the top inspecting another leak.' He ushered her through, shushing the dogs, and shooing them away to stop them jumping up at her.

'That's OK. Once I heard the dogs, I knew someone would come eventually!' She smiled back at him, feeling a little brighter.

'Lady Susan is waiting for you in the yellow drawing room, Sir Geoffrey went to join her. Do come through.'

She nervously followed him, he appeared to be in a good mood, which she hoped indicated that Sir Geoffrey was in a good mood too. They seemed to walk through corridor, after corridor, all the while Ted chatting amiably, and Katherine following his mixed blue, green and almond coloured, tweed jacket clad back, beneath which was a country check shirt, a green wool tie and a paler green jumper. He was shod in his usual brogue footwear, above which were his honey coloured cords. He stopped briefly as he came to an imposing pair of double doors, turned and smiled at her. 'Don't look so worried, you'll be fine.' So why did she feel she was about to face a very tricky interview? He opened one door and stood back to allow her to walk past him and into the room.

'Katherine, lovely to see you again,' smiled Sir Geoffrey, rising to shake her hand and kiss her lightly on the cheek.

'It's nice to see you again too,' she replied cautiously, 'and you too Lady Susan.' She always felt like she should curtsey when she met Lady Susan who was an imposing figure, brimming with confidence. Slightly shorter than Katherine, she was well padded, with stout legs which protruded from her below-the-knee skirt. Lady Susan always wore a skirt, no matter what, never "slacks" as she referred to trousers. She'd been brought up in an aristocratic family, sent to finishing school and, after a stint doing The Season, had moved swiftly on to marrying Geoffrey, for he was not a Baronet until his father died. She was not the type who was willowy, graceful and doe like, but of the more stocky, jolly hockey sticks collective, a no nonsense character, who always wore her straight, grey, hair at just above the shoulder, pushed back by a black velvet Alice band. Skirts were always the same length and invariably of wool with some kind of check, and a cashmere twin set which coordinated with one or other of the colour's in her skirt, along with the obligatory pearl necklace and earrings. On her wedding finger was a slim gold band and an enormous sapphire surrounded by substantial diamonds, an engagement ring passed down through the generations on Sir Geoffrey's side. This was a formidable woman, who took no nonsense from anyone, including her husband.

Lady Susan smiled graciously at Katherine. 'Please do, sit.' She indicated to an ancient settee which, Katherine discovered, was even more uncomfortable than it looked. 'Tea?' Enquired Lady Susan lifting the fine, bone china tea pot.

'Yes please, that would be lovely, thank you.' There was silence whilst Lady Susan poured milk into the delicate, rosebud painted cups and poured the tea through a strainer. Ted perched next to her and whilst they waited, continued to discuss the latest leak, discovered in the house with Sir Geoffrey. Katherine observed Sir Geoffrey, who was animated when the conversation turned to anything about the Estate. He was not much taller than his wife and barely an inch taller than Katherine. He was slim built, erring on the thin side, with thinning short, grey, hair and a pristinely brushed, bristly little grey moustache above his lip. It stuck straight out on each side and Katherine wondered how long it took him to groom it to stay in place. He had been brought up in the "stiff upper lip" generation, not showing his emotions or affections, always wore a jacket, shirt and tie, never ever just an open neck shirt. His clothes were well cut, excellently tailored but slightly jaded after many decades of use. Despite his brusqueness with his wife, Katherine liked to think that underneath he had a real affection for his wife.

'So, Katherine, Ted tells me that the police have kept you up to date about this jolly awful show at the farmhouse. Jolly bad luck that, eh?'

'Well, er, yes.' She wasn't quite sure she would call the death of someone "jolly bad luck" but having met Sir Geoffrey several times, she got the gist of his use of the English Language.

'Tell me then, Katherine, what do you know?' he peered intently at her with his slightly faded green eyes.

'I don't know if there is anything else I can tell you. I've told Ted what the police have told me and I've not heard anything further from them.'

'Well, where exactly were the remains found?' Lady Susan's cup rattled as her hand trembled when her husband said this.

'It was in the fireplace, the one that's at the end of the house, not the central fireplace. It had been bricked up. It was only when all the brambles and ivy had been pulled away that we realized there was another fireplace there. It had been impossible to see. I was hoping that there might be another nice inglenook fireplace and it could be opened up. Only a few bricks were taken out so that we could have a look, of course we got more than we bargained for when we did peer through the gap.'

He looked thoughtful before speaking again. 'What did you see when you looked through the gap in the bricks?'

'Um, well I only glanced, it was a skeleton, you know, a skull, that was all I saw. We called the police immediately. I've not been allowed back into the house since.'

'But,' interrupted Lady Susan, 'was there anything else there?'

Katherine looked confused. 'Sorry? I don't understand, like what?'

Momentarily Lady Susan looked flustered before regaining her composure. 'Anything, really, anything at all.'

'I didn't see anything else. The best people to ask are the police. I would imagine they will come and see you as you owned the property at the time the murder was committed.'

'Yes, yes, quite right, they're coming later this afternoon. Some detective chappy telephoned.' They lapsed into silence again. Katherine sipping her tea cautiously, trying her hardest not to make a slurping sound or show herself up in any way.

'Right, well, if you don't know anything more then so be it. Might come and have a look round when the builders start up again.' The assumption was there that Katherine would be agreeable to this and she wasn't about to upset the man who had just sold her, what had been and she hoped still would be, her dream home.

Taking this as her cue to depart, she thanked them for the cup of tea and followed Ted back to the front door.

'So,' he said, his hand on the front door handle. He smiled and hesitated. Yet again Katherine got the impression there was something he wanted to say, but couldn't bring himself to do so. 'Well, thanks for coming and I'll no doubt see you in the village sometime.'

'Quite possibly, thanks.' He held the door open for her. 'Bye,' she called as she went down the steps.

'Goodbye,' he replied, watching her get into her car and drive off.

She saw him in her mirror, standing, staring after her as she drove off and puzzled about what he hadn't said. When she reached the end of the long and winding drive she paused, then decisively turned left rather than right which would take her directly back into the village bringing her out into a lane close to the green. Instead she'd decided to drive past her farmhouse, after a short distance she turned left again into the single track lane, round a few bends and then saw the rickety entrance gate and moments later glimpsed her house, not busy with builders restoring it but people dressed in white, alien looking suits, coming and going in and around the house, forensics she guessed, though she wondered why they were back there again. She pulled up slowly and stopped by the entrance to the drive and observed a man and a woman who were gesticulating wildly at a uniformed policeman, who appeared to not be giving them the answers they were after. She didn't see the other policeman until he tapped on her window. She put it down a fraction.

'Sorry Madam, but I must ask you to move on. You are not allowed to stop here.'

'Yes, I will, I know, I mean I own the house.'

The policeman stared intently at her. She could almost hear him thinking "yeah and I've heard that one before" but instead he simple said 'Really?'

Katherine felt a frisson of irritation. It was her house, he could at least believe her. 'Yes. I'm Katherine Muier. I know I can't stop here, but I just wanted to see my house. If you don't believe me, check with D.I. Allix,' she said truculently.

'Ah, yes, sorry Mrs Muier, but we have had quite a few people turning up and claiming they own the house and they just need to pop inside. It's incredible the lengths people will go to.'

Katherine felt outraged. How dare other people try and gain access to her house and how dare they claim that it is their's! In amongst her indignation she felt slightly guilty for having been so brusque with the officer, as he was only doing his job and was ultimately protecting her property. She changed the subject slightly. 'Who are those people over there?' she asked indicating to the couple who were still giving the other police officer a hard time and, now that she had the window open could hear raised voices.

'That's Mr & Mrs Stillingfleet.'

'Oh! The girl's parents.' She could understand why they were so het up. 'Poor things.' The officer said nothing. 'I'd better go, thanks.' He gave a brief nod and said goodbye. She drove off, her heart aching for the distraught parents, imagining how she would feel if it were her daughter who had been murdered, perhaps a minuscule blessing of not being able to have children meant that she would never run the risk of ever knowing.

Chapter Seven

Two more work days passed and nothing further from the police. As a pale golden sun shone weakly through on the Saturday morning Katherine felt out of sorts, she couldn't settle to any particular task, she was too restless. Eventually she decided that she had to go out, she couldn't stand being stuck inside any longer and thought that now was the time to face the inevitable, get it over and done with rather than having it hanging over her like a black cloud. She'd been aware of a certain amount of curtain twitching every time she came and went at her rented terrace, it was time to face the music and let the gossips do their worst. She picked up her phone, purse, keys and a jute bag and headed into the village to the Farmer's Market which was held every Saturday morning in the village hall.

Feeling a little as though she was throwing herself into the lion's den, she felt in some masochistic way she was almost looking forward to it. She enjoyed living on her own, having given such a large chunk of her life from a relatively young age to looking after her husband and worrying about his needs, but from time to time she felt incredibly lonely and isolated and when it overwhelmed her she had a desperate need to be with others. Katherine knew she could always rely on her friends, but felt acutely that at weekends it was family time, a time for families to catch up together and she didn't want to intrude.

Katherine felt self-conscious walking through the estate to the main road, feeling as though all eyes were on her, when in fact she knew they probably weren't. She continued along the footpath and just before the post office crossed the road, walked across the grass and joined the road which went all around the perimeter of the green, the green being on her right and the primary school and playing fields on her left, a few steps later and she was at the village hall. A steady stream of people seemed to be coming and going and there was a large sign outside to match the one at the bottom of the green, by the main road, which announced "Farmer's Market Today 10 a.m. to 12 noon." She smiled nervously at the people who walked past her in the opposite direction, they smiled back but there was no hint of recognition. She began to realize how stupid she had been. Why on earth would anyone know who she was? How vain of me to even think that I would be the talk of the village, she felt foolish and ashamed.

There was a buzz of activity inside the hall, which was relatively modern having been built only five years previously to replace the rotting old building which had sufficed as a village hall prior to that. From what she could see there were about twenty or thirty stalls selling different produce and products, all seemingly local. The stall with the longest queue was the bread stall, everyone was standing patiently, chatting to one another and whilst she hated queues she was curious to discover what was so magical about this particular range of bread which made people queue so harmoniously? It also occurred to her that if she delayed joining the queue, the bread may have run out.

She stood quietly in line, listening in to the idle chit chat which was carrying on around her. Nobody seemed particularly curious or interested in her and she felt herself relax, she didn't feel like she was going to face the Spanish Inquisition after all. She tried to peer round those in front of her to see the different types of bread on display, they did look good, a large variety of flours were used to produce interesting looking and tantalizingly tasty bread. Not just your standard brown or white. There was rye flour bread, spicy bread, oat bread, a mix of different flour bread, bread with cheese and onion in it, olive bread, caraway seeded bread and many more, the selection was impressive and in addition to them, there was also a delectable array of mouthwatering cakes and pastries on offer. With a limited selection left by the time she reached the head of the queue, she settled for an oat mix bread, a 'meaty' looking croissant and an unadventurous doughnut. Katherine then decided to have a cup of coffee as refreshments were being served at one end of the light and airy hall. She was impressed that it was freshly brewed coffee and not out of a jar. She took her cup and sat at the only free table left, there was a buzz of conversation around her. Katherine sat and observed the ebb and flow of the market and sipped the piping hot coffee.

Behind her, several tables had been put together and a posse of people had gathered, regulars, she assumed by the way they greeted each other. She caught snatches of their conversation, though she wasn't really listening. Katherine finished her coffee and took it to the counter for washing up, it was only when she turned around that she came face to face with Betty, her heart sank.

'Kitty!' Betty eyed her with delight. 'How lovely to see you, I haven't seen you round the village, but I suppose that's understandable what with all that's been going on up at your house. Let me get you another cup of coffee.' Katherine tried to protest but found she was fighting a losing battle, before she knew it the coffee had been ordered and she had been propelled to the long table. The mix of older men and women sitting there eyed the interloper with suspicion. 'This is Kitty,' introduced Betty, 'she owns Wynenden Farmhouse.' She announced this triumphantly, as though holding up a gold medal at the Olympics. There was a collective inward gasp, followed by a babble of "oh, do come and sit here dear, come on make space," as they jostled amongst one another to get the top prize of sitting next to her.

Katherine looked round wildly, desperately hoping for some form of escape, but there was none forthcoming. Just as a black widow spider entices its partner back into its web, only for it to eat her mate, so she felt she was being irreversibly drawn into theirs. They crowded round her. 'So,' said Betty when she was settled, 'tell us exactly what has been happening at the farmhouse?'

About fifteen eager faces were focused on her. 'Well, um, I would imagine you know what I know,' she stuttered.

Betty clicked her tongue in a disapproval. 'Come on, I'm sure you know far more than we do! It is your house. Did you find the remains? Where was it? What did it look like?'

If ever there were a freak show, this was it and Katherine felt like she was the freak. 'I … Well … It was scary,' she was frantically trying to think of as many words and phrases as she could, which would make them believe she was telling them something important, but without actually divulging anything. There was a collective "ooh" at this. 'Yes. It was terrifying.' This produced lots of nodding and patting of her hands. 'We had to call the police right away.'

'Oh, course, of course,' muttered one.

'Absolutely, very wise,' murmured another.

'They were very quick.' She glanced around at them realizing that if she paused after each small statement, it appeared to have a more dramatic effect on them. 'They were very efficient.' Pause. 'There were detectives and uniformed policemen and suited forensics people.' She gave another pause. 'They're very busy.' She stopped. They looked at her eagerly. She suddenly had an idea. 'Tell me,' she said to her captive audience. 'What happened ten years ago? Were you all here? Did you help with the search?' She hoped that by deflecting back on to them, she would take the pressure off herself. It seemed to work, they all started talking at once, but Betty, having brought the prize to the table, seemed to be unofficially in charge.

Happy to be in the spot light, she started. 'We were all here. It was dreadful. Well, in fact to start with, we didn't believe Cecilia's parents. They said she'd gone missing, but she was a bit of a wild thing.'

'You can say that again,' interrupted her neighbour.

'And she'd been away you see. No one saw her from Easter until October. Of course they said she'd gone on an educational trip to stay with a relative in France.' Betty glanced round and, as if on cue, there was a lot of rolling of the eyes and muttering.

'You don't think she did then?' asked Katherine, intrigued.

'Who knows? There were rumours.' She paused as though contemplating what to say next. 'But no one really knew. Then she was back, we only saw her for a few days and then she disappeared. Of course we all thought she'd been sent away again. That's why no one believed her parents when they said she had gone missing. And also, she had been known to just disappear for a day or two previously, and back she'd come as though nothing had happened. So it was a good week or so before any of us took them seriously. Once the police got involved and started asking questions we realized maybe there *was* something wrong.'

'So what happened next?' prompted Katherine.

'Well, we did what all villages do in a time of crisis, we pulled together. We had search parties out all over the village and surrounding fields and woodland. Sir Geoffrey got Ted, who was his new Estate Manager then, to coordinate searches on the Estate, he was most insistent that we keep going. Even when we had searched and searched, he made the staff up at the Estate keep searching. Day after day, from dawn 'til dusk, for two whole weeks.'

'Really?' Katherine was surprised.

'Yes. He just wouldn't give up. As time went on we began to wonder if something awful had really happened to her. There was just no sign of her. After several months, when there was still no sign of her, we all concluded that maybe something horrid had happened to her. No matter

what a person is like, they don't deserve to be murdered.'
She shook her head sadly as others agreed with her.

They lapsed into silence, which was eventually broken
by a rotund, elderly woman with a tight blue-rinse perm,
wearing a synthetic red jumper and a rather large mole on
her right cheek which sprouted numerous thick dark hairs.
'She was a bit of a madam though.' There was a silence,
before there were quiet murmurings of "true, true". 'She
gave her parents the right run-around and with her having
gone to that posh school up the road too!'

'What? Wynenden School?' Katherine was suddenly
alert. That was where Libby's children were, at the Prep
School.

'Yes, that's the one. Right snobby lot up there. Flashing their money around, driving round in their four wheel
drives like they own the place.'

Katherine felt herself bristle with anger. It always irritated her when people made stereotypical judgements of
the children at private schools and their parents who sent
them there. It was assumed that, if the parents sent their
children to such a school, they were snobby and full of
themselves and loaded in cash. In fact, from Katherine's
experience - though it varied from school to school - the
majority were far from that. She knew some parents
worked two jobs, just so that their child/children could attend such a school, wanting to give their child or children
the best education they could. Many sacrificed going out,
holidays, new cars, new clothes, in order to give them a
private education. In some cases, grandparents paid for
their grandchildren to attend such schools. Whilst there
always would be an element of overtly wealthy parents,
this did not automatically make them snobby, rude or arro-

gant. Katherine knew that you got that in all walks of life, whether you sent your child to a private school or a state school. The selfish attitude seen today in many an adult, and inevitably their offspring, was a symptom of the me, me, me society in which they now lived.

Seemingly unaware of the effect her comments on Katherine had had, the woman continued to prattle on, gaining confidence as her audience listened. 'Her parents have got a lot to answer for. They think they own this village from the way they behave. They live in their average detached house behind their silly electric gates. No manners, not like Sir Geoffrey and his wife, now they've got true breeding,' she sat back smugly.

Katherine didn't want to listen to any more of this. It was spiteful and hurtful and probably not true. She didn't know the Stillingfleet's, but no matter what they were like as individuals, they should still be shown compassion at a time like this.

'Well, thanks for the coffee,' she said doing her utmost not to appear rude, 'but I would really like to have a look at the stalls before they pack up, it's 11.30 already.' She forced a smile on her face and thanked them again. There was a cheery goodbye from them all, but Katherine was sure that, as soon as she was out of earshot, she would be subject to a discussion. What was her fate to be? Liked or reviled? She wasn't sure if she really cared.

The stalls turned out to be an interesting mix. Katherine bought cheese and milk from a local farmer, ham and chicken breasts from another, honey from a local apiarist, vegetables from an elderly couple who grew the produce themselves, apple juice from another and, finally, a delectable looking lemon cupcake, with perfect lemon butter icing, sprinkled with glitter, from a young mum trying to a earn a little money whilst being a full time mum to a toddler, Saturday being one of the morning's when she could leave the toddler with her husband. Laden with her goodies Katherine weaved her way purposefully towards the door, endeavouring not to glance in the direction of the group she had been sitting with. Glimpsing down for a moment, she bumped into someone. 'Oh, sorry!' She exclaimed, looking up, only to see that it was Ted smiling down at her.

'Hi! How are you? You look like you've been busy single-handedly keeping the market in business!'

'Thought I'd do my bit! I have to say, I'm very impressed. I was expecting a couple of stalls with a few moulding vegetables on them and nothing else.'

'We're lucky, it is a good one, some of the others round here don't have as many stalls and are not doing so well. It's a vicious circle, stall holders are there to earn a living and need people to come in to buy, if the markets don't get the stallholders, people don't continue to visit and of course if there aren't interesting stalls selling good produce and products, people won't come. Fortunately, the one here is thriving. It's been going for about five years now.'

'I'll certainly be back. There are a few stalls I didn't get to, lots of people gathering round them and I'm a bit laden down, besides I didn't want to get caught again.'

'Caught?' he looked quizzically at her, his head cocked to one side.

'They're only being friendly. Betty from the post office and some other people from the village.'

'Sitting on the long table at the back,' he grinned.

'Yes. How did you know?'

'They're always there. Woe betide anyone who tries to sit at their table uninvited! I guess they mean well. I think some of them are lonely and this is the highlight of their week.'

Katherine felt a twinge, she knew what loneliness was like, that's what had propelled her to the market in the first place. Her face must have flickered with something which Ted saw and recognized in himself. A bachelor himself, having never married, he'd broken up with his long term girlfriend over a year ago. She'd wanted commitment, he was happy as they were and whilst, in hindsight, it had been the right decision to part company - for he could see that his reluctance to commit was down to his lack of strong feelings for her - he had times when he too felt lonely. All his friends were married, some divorced and on their second marriage, it was an isolating world being older and single sometimes.

Impulsively he spoke. 'I don't suppose, if you are free tonight, you'd fancy meeting for a drink would you?' he blushed a bit as he asked.

Caught off guard, it had been a long time since someone had asked her out on a date and not something she had been actively searching for. She blushed a little too. ' Oh. Um...'

'Sorry. It's presumptuous of me, you must be busy, forget I asked,' he blustered on.

'No. No I am not actually. That would be nice, I don't really know any of the pubs round here. Though perhaps we could give The Speckled Goose a miss, bit too local for me at the moment!' She gave a slight smile.

His face lit up. 'Of course! I'll have a think. Would you like to meet at the pub or can I pick you up?' He didn't want to be too forward, quite ridiculous he thought, for a man of forty-two in this day and age of internet dating and the apparent easy come and easy go attitude to dating and sex.

'Um.' She hesitated again, weighing up the pros and cons of being picked up, verses meeting there. The advantage of meeting there being she could leave when she wanted to, if the evening went pear shaped. But on the other hand she knew Ted, he wasn't someone she'd picked off a dating site, and he was perfectly pleasant and a gentleman, so she should be able to trust him. 'If you could pick me up, that would be lovely, thank you. Say about 8 p.m.?'

'Great! I'll see you then.' They bade farewell until later and Katherine walked home feeling slightly lighter and with a grin on her face. She was impressed that at forty-seven, she still got asked out and by a younger man too!

Of course, as the evening drew nearer, Katherine began to feel apprehensive about what lay ahead. After all, the last time she had been asked out, was thirty years ago when Rex had first asked her out on a date. And look what a disaster that eventually turned out to be, she muttered to herself. Her friends had all tried to fix her up on blind dates, which she had refused. She would rather stay at home and stick pins in her eyes, than go out on a blind date. They'd also done the usual trick of holding a dinner party and seating her next to the only single male at the dinner. Each occasion turned out to be unique and not always in a positive way. Eventually her friends got the message to leave her to her own devices and she had settled into her single life, on the whole quite contentedly. What was the protocol these days? Society seemed so promiscuous, she sincerely hoped that she wasn't expected to leap into bed on the first date with any man who happened to ask her out. Maybe she should have met him there? Several times she came close to picking up the phone and arranging to meet him at whichever pub they were going to, but chickened out each time.

By 7.30 p.m. she was ready. She'd settled on a pair of sage coloured, slim fitting, needle cord trousers (in case he had wandering hands, a skirt may be too inviting), a cotton scoop neck, slim fitting, thin double-layer top in damson with a stripy green and damson under-layer, along with a damson coloured cashmere cardigan, and her feet were shod with a pair of low heeled, dark tan, slim fitting, riding style boots. She wore simple diamond stud earrings and a white gold pendant with a tiny diamond in it. She thought she looked smart, rather than scruffy. Not overdressed, nor underdressed, for the evening, though worried that possibly she was being a bit safe and dull, in her bid to avoid being overtly sexy.

8 p.m. prompt brought his knock on the door. She opened it and smiled. 'Hi.'

'You ready?' he asked, eyeing her appreciatively.

'Absolutely.' She slipped on her navy pea coat, scooped her glossy chestnut hair, from under the collar, and closed the door behind her, all the while admiring the jeans, casual shirt and plain jacket he was wearing. She caught a waft of something lovely and citrusy and spicy.

He held the door of his freshly washed green Land Rover Discovery, closed it behind her and walked round to the driver's side. 'I thought we'd go to The Grouse & Peacock. It's about 3 miles away in the Cranbrook direction. Should be far enough away from the locals, though anywhere round here you're likely to bump into someone you know.'

'Sounds fine. Not been there before.' They lapsed into silence, interspersed with the odd polite comment regarding the weather or the countryside they were passing. The Grouse & Peacock turned out to be in the middle of nowhere, down several little lanes. But despite this, the car park was packed. It was an old sixteenth century building, with low beams and a couple of log fires burning merrily away. Not for the first time, Katherine was glad that smoking had been banned. It made for a far more pleasant experience in her opinion. She didn't have to choke on hideous cigarette smoke all evening and come home with her clothes and hair stinking of it.

'It looks lovely,' she commented as they weaved their way through the throng towards the bar. Ted spotted a tiny table with two chairs unoccupied near one of the fires.

'Here. Have a seat,' he said pulling the chair out for her. 'What would you like to drink?'

'A glass of white wine please. Something like a sauvignon blanc if they have it.' He disappeared off to the bar leaving Katherine to observe the clientele in the pub. There seemed to be a whole mix of ages, from those who seemed too young - in her eyes - to even be in a pub, all the way up through the middle aged, like herself, and on to the elderly. Quite a few seemed to know Ted and he appeared to be chatting amiably to them whilst waiting his turn at the bar.

'Sorry about that, bit too busy tonight. Not usually quite this hectic on a Saturday night.' He sat down. 'Cheers!' He said raising his glass of ginger beer.

'Cheers!' she responded, taking a sip of her wine. It was fresh, delicious, citrusy, zingy, just the way she liked it. 'You not even having one drink?' She'd assumed he would have had one alcoholic drink, even though he was driving. Personally, she never had an alcoholic drink if she were driving, but was realistic about other people having a different opinion on this matter.

'No. Don't drink. Never have done.'

'Really?' she was surprised 'Why?'

He shrugged. 'Seeing most of my mates getting plastered from a young age, acting like idiots, throwing up and generally being complete morons, kind of put me off.' He grinned.

'Ah, well. Don't worry, I'm not going to get like that!' She now felt rather self-conscious sipping her wine.

His face fell. 'Oh! I didn't mean anything by it really!' He said hastily. 'It's a free country and everyone's entitled to do what they want.'

She relaxed a little. 'I don't drink if I'm driving, never have done, never will. I think one alcoholic drink is too many when driving. Of course, most people don't see it like that and are happy to drink and drive.'

Ted grimaced. 'I know what you mean. They just don't see what the consequences can be…,' his voice trailed off.

They sat awkwardly in silence for a few moments. 'So,' said Katherine breaking the silence, 'what made you become a Land Agent?'

'Easy,' he smiled. 'I've loved being outside since I was tiny. I grew up on a farm surrounded by countryside, loved it. The rolling hills, the fresh air, changing seasons, could never imagine working in an office 24/7, I'd feel too cooped up. With this job there is such variety, there's always something different going on, problems to solve.' He looked contented.

'If you grew up on a farm, did you not want to be a farmer? Take over the family farm or something?'

'No. I loved the farm, but I knew I didn't want to be a farmer. It's relentless and I also knew that my elder brother would always take over the family farm. I'm still involved in farming because of the farm on the Estate, but it's not the day in, day out, farming that the farmer has to deal with. I don't think I'm explaining myself very well?' He raised an eyebrow in question at her.

'I think you are. I suppose there's the farm, the house, the properties, managing the budgets and all that sort of thing, which your job entails?'

'Pretty much. Coming up with new and innovative ways to increase income just to maintain the main house, is constant. You've seen it. It needs major work on it. You'd need several million, just to do the basics at the moment, as soon as we plug one problem, another occurs. Bit like trying to stop a sieve from leaking,' he grinned ruefully.

'There must be loads of different ways to raise money? It's such a beautiful house. Can't it be opened to the public?'

Ted rolled his eyes. 'Don't start! I agree with you, but it's not my house, if you know what I mean. Oh no!' he groaned.

'What? What is it?'

'Don't look round.'

Of course, the instant he said this, she wanted to. 'Why not?'

'Andrew Battle's just walked in. If we keep a low profile, he might not see us.'

'Oh no.' She echoed his earlier sentiment. 'He's the last person I want to see. Did I tell you he came over to the farmhouse again? Shortly before the works began. He was, yet again, trying to persuade me to sell up. Being all smarmy, saying things like "you really don't want to be worrying your pretty little head about something like this" and "an enchanting woman like you must be far too busy to bother with such a big project," it was hideous.'

'I can imagine.' He grimaced in sympathy.

'I don't understand why he's so desperate for me to sell? He even added a further ten percent on top of the ridiculous sum he'd previously offered me.'

'You didn't accept did you?' he asked sharply.

Surprised by his tone, she bristled. 'No! Of course I didn't! I would never sell to him and besides, as you are well aware, I agreed as part of the terms of my purchasing the farmhouse, never to sell to him and I won't. I told him as much too.'

'Sorry. I didn't mean to be brusque. It's just I know how strongly Sir Geoffrey feels about that man. He absolutely loathes him. It would probably kill him if it ended up in Andrew's hands.'

'I know he's an unpleasant man. But why does Sir Geoffrey feel so strongly?'

Ted Shrugged. 'No idea.'

'Ah! What do we have here?' They winced as Andrew's foghorn voice boomed at them. 'Having a lovely drink together. Plotting some plan together? Is that how you got the house Kitty? Did you do favours?' He leered at her.

'How dare you!' shouted Ted, leaping up in her defence. 'Just because you are such a low life, doesn't mean that

71

everyone else is. Don't judge people by your own standards.' He was quite red in the face with fury and the pub had fallen silent. Ted sat down as quickly as he had leapt up, embarrassed at drawing attention to himself.

'Touched a sore spot have I? Didn't come up with the goods? Never mind, better luck next time. My offer still stands Kitty, despite the gruesome goings on up there.' With that he sauntered off in a cloud of cloying aftershave to a young woman in a short skirt, low top and surgically enhanced breasts.

'Don't,' she whispered to Ted. Grabbing his arm before he could leap up and punch him. 'He's not worth it. If he can't get his own way, he'll do everything to rile the other person. Leave it. He's really not worth it,' she reiterated.

Ted scowled at him. 'Sorry.'

'What for? You were my knight in shining armour! Thanks. Made a change for someone else to step in for me. He's an awful, awful man. Come on, let's not allow him to spoil our evening. I'll get some drinks. Another ginger beer or do you want to throw caution to the wind and have a sparkling mineral water?' she grinned at him.

He laughed. 'Surprise me!' he replied.

Chapter Eight

The phone rang persistently, interrupting Katherine's delicious sleep. She fumbled for the handset. Picked it up and mumbled into the receiver. 'Hello?'

'Oh, sorry Kitty. Did I wake you?' It was Libby.

Katherine yawned and glanced at the clock – 8.00 a.m. Why was it, that people with children just assumed that everyone else was up at the crack of dawn at the weekend? 'S'OK, what's up?'

'I thought you might like to come to lunch today? We didn't get much of a chance to catch up last Wednesday and the children would love to see you.'

'That'd be nice. Thanks.'

'Great! 12 o'clock do? Do you think you'll have been able to drag yourself out of bed by then?' she giggled.

'Hah, hah. You know I don't often have a lie in and it is only 8 o'clock and it is Sunday!'

'Just joking. Jealousy really. Never get to have a lie in these days. Anyway, see you later. Bye.' The phone clicked and Katherine flopped back down onto her pillow, pulled the duvet up and snuggled back down for a bit more kip.

Katherine beetled through the countryside later that morning, having thoroughly enjoyed a luxuriant lie in and a lazy breakfast. She reflected on the previous evening, which had made a pleasant change. Ted was good company. Fun, witty and relaxed, once Andrew had left the pub half an hour after his little performance. She scowled as she remembered him. Pesky man, she thought. Ted had filled her in a bit, on Andrew's background. Born and bred locally, he grew up on a local council estate with his mother and sisters, his abusive father having left when he was five years old. He'd left school with no qualifications and had started doing odd jobs and a bit of wheeler dealing from a young age. If there was a scam going on, he was usually behind it. Somehow, he had then managed to find enough money to buy a wreck of a terrace. Did it up and sold it on for a substantial profit. Then he did another and then another and another. Next he started doing the properties up, keeping them, and then renting them. After that, he moved into commercial property to diversify, and in conjunction with this were his sidelines. Basically, anything he could make money out of. Apparently this was all common knowledge and was what Andrew constantly bragged about. It would appear that he had done very well for himself. He'd bought a scrappy, derelict, bungalow in 7 acres on the edge of the village. Got planning permission, knocked it down and built a huge, flash new house with several garages, where he kept his collection of expensive cars. He worked hard and he played hard. Whilst Katherine respected and applauded hard work, she was not sure how ethically he worked, nor how legally, but that was pure speculation on her part.

She arrived at Libby's house and pulled up in front of the magnificent Tudor house, surrounded by its manicured lawns. Libby had worked for years in the city. Long hours, good pay and substantial bonuses. Unlike her colleagues, who blew their bonuses on flash cars and fast living, she had saved her bonuses. And by the time she eventually met her future husband, James, had a tidy sum tucked away to ensure - if she were wise and not extravagant with it - she need never work again. James too worked in the city, with good pay but not quite the astronomical level of bonuses which Libby had received. After a swift courtship they were married, and this was quickly followed by the arrival of Henry, now eight, and subsequently Alice, now 6. In ten years, her life had changed from work obsessed single woman who, at 36, felt she would never marry and have children, to domesticated wife and mother, living in the country, yet another huge change to the London life she had lived for so long. For Katherine it was wonderful that her best friend from school had moved out from London and was living so close and now, having moved to Wynenden, Katherine found herself only seven miles away from her friend. But despite their wealth and their comfortable lifestyle, Libby did not take it foregranted. Her parents had had a constant struggle with money, often going without, so that Libby could have extra lessons to help her academically, and even more so when she went on to university. She had done the comprehensive school she attended - and her parents - proud by getting into Oxford University and Katherine had been so very proud of her best friend's achievements.

'Kitty!' Two small figures ran out of the front door and flung themselves at her, their blond heads burying themselves into her.

She squeezed them tightly to her and kissed their heads. Hi, you two! It's so lovely to see you. Let me have a look at you. She held them away from her, squinted at them closely. 'Yup, I'm absolutely sure! You've most definitely grown since I last saw you!' - which had only been three weeks previously. The children swelled with pride at the complement.

'Come on.' They dragged her by her hands. 'Can you come and play with us?' they pleaded.

'Let poor Kitty get her coat off first!' reprimanded their father good naturedly as he kissed her on both cheeks.

'Good to see you Kitty. You're looking well.' He peeled the children away from her, who then ran ahead yelling to their mother that Kitty had arrived.

'They are such lovely children.' She gazed after them fondly. She adored seeing her Godchildren, they brought such joy and, in some small way, helped fill a tiny corner of the empty feeling she had, from not being able to have had children.

'Hmm,' replied James, 'they have their moments!'

She laughed. Looking into his good natured face, bags under his eyes from overwork, but crinkles round them from laughter. His short blond hair was tousled and slightly wild.

'Kitty!' Libby came out of the kitchen, wiping her hands on a tea towel. She kissed and hugged her friend. 'I'm afraid you are not going to get any peace until you play with them!'

'I know. Don't worry! I don't mind crawling around on the floor and playing whatever it is they want to.'

Libby eyed the knee length, suede, skirt Katherine was wearing. 'In that? Are you sure?'

Katherine laughed. 'I'll manage somehow. Don't worry!' She headed off to the playroom. It was a ritual which she enjoyed. As soon as she arrived, she dived off to play with the children. This kept the children happy and prevented the constant nagging of "will you play with me?" for the rest of the afternoon, which drove their parents mad. Katherine didn't mind. After all, she wasn't with them twenty-four hours a day, seven days a week.

A few moments later James wandered in carrying a mug of coffee. 'Thought you might need this.' He raised the mug at her and put it down onto a mat on the windowsill.

'Thanks,' she replied, delving deep and swishing around in a large box of Lego. He left them to it and went to help his wife with the lunch.

An hour later, they were all seated round the large kitchen table, enjoying a full Sunday roast lunch. The works, with roast beef, Yorkshire Pudding, numerous vegetables and gravy, to be followed by homemade apple pie and custard. The children munched happily having had an hour with their favourite adult (after their parents of course) and her undivided attention. They were eager to get back and finish the challenge which Katherine had set them – to build the largest castle they possibly could, with stables, barns and anything else she could think of to keep them busy – and had to be chided by their parents to not gobble their food down. The conversation flowed easily between the five of them and, with apple pie finished, the children raced off to continue with their Lego and Libby and Katherine abandoned James to do the clearing and washing up and settled themselves by the fire in the sitting room with their mugs of coffee.

'So, tell me, what's the latest?' asked Libby.

Succinctly, Katherine brought her up to speed ending with the information that Cecilia had been a pupil at Wynenden School.

'No! Really? Gosh!' Libby was rather at a loss for words.

'I don't suppose you'd heard anything about her had you?'

'No. There's no reason why I should have.'

'I know, but I just wondered? You know how people gossip and this is a pretty hot topic. There must be a few people up there who knew her, maybe even teachers who taught her?'

'I suppose, but they would be at the Senior School.'

'Hmm.'

'Hmm, what?' asked Libby.

'Oh, I don't know. I guess I'm curious. I can't get my head around the fact that somebody would murder a six-teen year old child, I mean I know she wasn't strictly a child, but she was barely an adult. How could anybody do such a thing?'

Libby shook her head and shivered. 'I don't know. It's too horrible to think about. Do you know anything about her?'

'Not really, only what those women were gossiping about. But it just seems, so, so ..., so local I suppose. That sounds stupid, but I can't help feeling that whoever killed her, must be close by. I mean, that house hadn't been lived in for a good twenty years or so when she was murdered.

And it's not exactly in a location where you would just happen to pass by, it's so tucked away. Whoever killed her *must* have known the area. Wouldn't you think?'

'Yes. I think they must have. It seems unlikely they would happen across the house by chance, but I suppose you never know.'

'And to have gone to such lengths to brick her body up in an old fireplace. You must be talking pre-meditated, wouldn't you think?'

'I don't know.'

'Well, the average person doesn't just happen to have bricks and mortar and everything you need to murder and then brick up a body on them, do they?' Libby shook her head in response.

'Any more coffee?' enquired James carrying a tray with his mug, milk, a cafetiere and a box of chocolate truffles on it.

'Please.' They both replied.

'You two look deep in thought,' he commented, flopping down onto one of the sofas and stretching his legs out. 'What are you talking about?'

'The girl. You know the one who was found?' replied his wife as she endeavoured to choose a truffle. Absent-mindedly they munched on them and brought him up to speed.

'You on a mission Kitty?' She looked questioningly at him. 'Too find out who did it? You becoming the new Miss Marple?' he smiled.

She snorted in laughter. 'You've got to be kidding haven't you?! I'm just curious. When something like that turns up in your house, you're bound to be. Don't you think?'

'True. So why do you think that house was chosen? You know, for the body?'

'Remote I guess. You're not going to be disturbed by anyone. Which brings me back to thinking it must be someone local. Someone who knew of the house, knew it was empty. It had to be.'

'What a horrible thought,' shivered Libby. 'To think that someone you may have passed in the street, did it.' She wriggled her shoulders in disgust.

'Horrible. Really horrible. But does that person still live around here? Or would they have scarpered soon after the murder?'

'Possibly. But if they thought they had got away with it, then there would be no reason to leave would there?' reasoned James.

'If that's the case, then what will they do now that she's been found? Is he, or she, a threat now?'

'What a hideous thought,' replied Libby. 'Whoever it is must be feeling vulnerable. I mean, it's amazing what the police can discover these days. Even the tiniest speck of something or other can lead to the discovery of the killer.'

'So says the expert.' James smiled indulgently at his wife. 'I think you've been watching too many crime drama's on TV.'

She threw a cushion at him. 'Don't be mean! And besides, Mr Great Authority On Such Things, how would you know?'

'Touché!'

'It's true though. There may be a clue there. Something the police find, I mean that's why they're ripping the house to bits.'

'They're not are they?' asked Libby tucking into another truffle.

'Well, I don't know. Who knows what they are doing. I can't get in there. The saving grace is that the house was being ripped to bits anyway, so hopefully they won't be doing anything the builders wouldn't have been doing.'

'The question you have to ask,' James' mind was whirring away now, 'is why? Why was she killed?'

'Good point, darling'

'Yes. Why indeed?' Thoughtfully Katherine twiddled some of her hair round and round her fingers. 'If you have the motive, then maybe you will find the murderer?'

'Definitely think you have been watching the same programs as Libby, Kitty! It might have been totally random, maybe some paedophile or something.'

'Oh, don't say that James! I hate even hearing mention of such sicko's. It fills me with dread and makes me want to surround the children in cotton wool and never let them go out.'

'I know. I feel the same,' he replied, 'but it is a possibility.'

'The only personality trait those women really came up with, was that Cecilia was a bit "wild". But I suppose it depends what their definition of wild is? Do they mean someone who doesn't always say "please" or "thank you" or do they mean someone who's off partying every night and joy riding around the village?'

'Hmm. I'm sure that Betty woman at your village shop would know more. You could always ask her and I could subtly ask around at school. Normally I try to keep out of the gossip loop, but there might be something useful there.'

'That's the problem, how do you know what's gossip and what's not?'

'The only people who can answer that, are those who are being gossiped about,' interjected James. 'And they may not even be aware that they are being gossiped about and if they are, they may see no reason to set people straight. Anyway, apart from the obvious Kitty, how is life treating you at the moment?'

Kitty smirked to herself, but not before Libby - who had known her for far too - long had noticed.

'Kitty,' she said slowly as though talking to a naughty two year old, 'what aren't you telling me?' She narrowed her eyes and peered at her friend. 'Come on. Out with it! Something's up. What is it?'

'Nothing!' she denied vehemently.

'Don't give me that! I know there's something,' she paused and then gasped as a thought struck her, 'it's a man isn't it!'

Katherine felt a slow, creeping, blush rise up her chest, neck and finally her face. Why on earth was she blushing? She wasn't dating anyone, she'd just happened to go out for a drink with a friend. Totally casual. Nothing to it. Or so she liked to convince herself. 'It's nothing, really, I just went out for a drink last night.'

'A drink? With whom?'

'Oh, no one really. Just a friend, no big deal.'

'If it was no big deal, why are you blushing?'

'Come on Libby. Give her a break. She doesn't have to tell you and besides who wouldn't blush with you interrogating them so ferociously?'

Katherine shot him a grateful glance.

'Hmm. I'm suspicious.'

'Well there's nothing to tell. I went out for a very casual drink. Had a pleasant evening, apart from that pest Andrew Battle making a nuisance of himself, and that was it. End of. Nothing to tell.'

Reluctantly, Libby decided not to pursue the line of questioning any further. There'd be time enough when she got Kitty on her own, without James sitting there giving her piercing glares to drop it.

Much to Katherine's relief, they changed the subject and spent the rest of the afternoon chatting about the children, work, the house and admiring the Lego structures the children had created.

Chapter Nine

Having refused offers of supper, Katherine had left Libby and James to calm their over excited children down and prepare them for a good night's sleep before school the next day. Feeling joyously happy for some reason, Katherine drove home humming to herself and parked up on the narrow driveway in front of her rented terrace. She eyed all the packed boxes, neatly lined up in the hallway and kitchen, and knew she had to get round to unpacking them, but really she couldn't be bothered. Why spoil a lovely relaxing day, she thought, and flung her coat on top of a pile in an attempt to hide them. Out of sight, out of mind, she told herself. Instead, she made a camomile tea, flopped down onto a sofa and switched the television on. Barely had she flicked through a couple of channels, when there was a loud and determined knock at the door. Who on earth was that? She groaned, reluctantly getting out of her comfy spot to answer it.

Standing on her doorstep were a couple who looked vaguely familiar, but whom she could not place. The man was tall, with a paunch, short grey hair and a pair of black rimmed glasses perched on his bulbous, porous, nose, which indicated - along with his ruddy complexion and broken capillaries - that he was a heavy drinker. Next to him stood a woman who looked a bit like mutton dressed as lamb. Her hair was heavily highlighted blonde and straightened to within an inch of its life, to below ear length, along with a sharp fringe and her clothes were tight and short, with high heels which seemed to make her wobble in the cool evening air.

'Can I help you?' enquired Katherine cautiously.

'I'm hoping you can,' replied the man in a gravelly voice, which also hinted that he was a smoker. This was backed up by a burst of phlegmy coughing. Katherine looked questioningly at him, waiting for him to stop. 'I'm Rupert Stillingfleet and this is my wife Audrey. We're Cecilia's parents.'

Now she knew why they looked vaguely familiar, this was the couple she had seen having a heated discussion with one of the policemen at her farmhouse. She hesitated, not keen to invite them in. 'What is it I can help you with?'

The couple looked at one another. 'Could we come in please?' asked Rupert.

Reluctantly, Katherine stepped back and showed them through to the sitting room. 'Please, take a seat.' She indicated to a sofa and then sat opposite them. 'I'm very sorry about your daughter.'

A slight sob came from Audrey, who pulled herself together, but sat there with the slight all-over tremble of a small dog. 'Thank you,' replied Rupert.
There was an awkward silence. 'So what is it I can do for you?'

'We really want to know more about what happened when our daughter was found? You were there I believe?' he looked questioningly at her.

Katherine squirmed uncomfortably. 'Yes I was, but there isn't really much to tell. I mean, the police must have told you everything?' She looked queryingly from one to the other, observing Audrey wringing her fingers.

'Of course they have. But please, go through, step by step, what happened. What you saw?' His brown eyes pleaded with her through his thick rimmed glasses and she caught an unpleasant waft of stale smoke and alcohol.

'Well. I was talking to my builder and one of the men was carefully removing bricks, from what we hoped would turn out to be a bricked up fireplace. When a few had been removed, he peered inside and then discovered, well discovered ...,' she struggled to find the right words, 'discovered your daughter. The police were called and we left the house until they arrived. That's it.'

'But what did you see?'

Katherine looked confused. 'What do you mean?'

'You looked. So what did you see?' he persisted.

'I um … Um. Saw your daughter. Briefly. Very briefly. That was it.'

'Was that all? Nothing else?'

'Nothing else, no.' She was puzzled and not sure where his line of questioning was going.

'Are you absolutely sure?' he said forcefully.

'Yes. Quite sure. Now if there's nothing else...' she tailed off hopefully.

Audrey Stillingfleet spoke for the first time, her voice was high and squeaky. 'She had a necklace. We gave it to her for her sixteenth birthday. It was gold with a gold butterfly on the chain, about the size of a fifty-pence piece. Was she wearing it?' Her green eyes were filled with so much pain and desperation that it made Katherine want to cry to look at her.

'I don't really know,' she said softly, 'I don't think there was anything like that. But the police might have found it, have you asked them?'

'Yes,' she whispered hoarsely, trying desperately not to cry again.

'If they've not found it, then it's probably not there. They're certainly doing a thorough search of the house.'

'Please,' she pleaded, 'please look for it.'

'I will ask the builders to keep an eye open for it. If they should find it, I will let you know, but I will have to let the police know first,' she replied kindly, knowing full well that if the police hadn't found it, there was no chance that she, or the builders, would.

'And you're quite sure there was nothing else?' interjected Rupert, staring so intently at her that Katherine felt like a criminal.

'No,' she replied firmly, standing up to indicate that she expected them to go.

They took the hint and got up too, on their way out Audrey's thin bony fingers grasped Katherine's. Desperately she looked at her. 'You'll let me know if you find it then?'

'Of course,' she replied.

Katherine shut the door behind them and closed her eyes. That was awful, she thought, and what on earth was Rupert going on about? Was he talking about the necklace? Whatever it was he gave her the creeps, she shivered to get rid of the picture of him in her mind and dropped herself down onto the sofa, feeling disgruntled. Why oh why had it had to happen at all? And why at the house she had just bought? Why couldn't life be straightforward sometimes? She belatedly realized she had missed an opportunity to ask them about their daughter. About what she had been like, she was sure it would have been a very different picture to the one which had already been painted to her. Feeling totally out of sorts, she took herself off for a nice relaxing bath and an early night.

Katherine immersed herself in work and did her best to forget about the murder investigation, but despite doing her utmost not to think about it, it kept popping in to her head. She couldn't get over her thought that Cecilia had been murdered by someone local, it had to be, she was convinced of it. It kept niggling away at her. If only the girl hadn't been found at the farmhouse, been found somewhere else, then she would barely have given it a second thought. But Cecilia hadn't. She had been found at her farmhouse and there was no getting away from it. Nipping in to the village shop to pick up a pint of milk on the way back from work one evening, she was caught by Betty.

'Kitty, how are you?' she enquired pleasantly.

'Oh, fine thanks and you?' Inside she was wrestling with her conscience. Should she ask Betty about Cecilia and risk being a gossip or should she just keep out of it, mind her own business and stop playing detective?

'Any news?' asked Betty hopefully.

'No, nothing, but I'm not likely to hear anything. I won't be told anything about the case. There's no reason I will be, only about when the builders can get back on site.'

Betty made her little tutting sound. 'It must be so frustrating for you to not be able to get on,' she paused.

Katherine took the opportunity and dived in. 'How about you? Have you heard anything? After all, you are at the centre of the village.' She smiled encouragingly at Betty.

'Well,' she paused looking round in the kind of "walls have ears" way, 'I don't like to speak ill of the dead...'

Katherine held her breath and continued to smile pleasantly.

'But there's a lot of talk around the village.'

'Really? Like what?' Katherine opened her eyes wide in innocence.

'About what Cecilia had been up to during those months when she had supposedly been in France with relatives.' Betty leaned forward towards Katherine and lowered her voice. 'They say that she was pregnant and was sent away to have an abortion and to get her away from her boyfriend.'

Katherine was shocked. 'Really? Gosh! So who was her boyfriend? Was he someone local?'

Betty nodded. 'Lovely boy, an absolute gem, soft as anything, but her parents didn't approve. They had high hopes for their daughter and didn't want her being led astray by a local lad. Didn't even try to get to know him. Just did all they could to keep them apart, but they seemed besotted with one another. Well he certainly did, she might have been going out with him to deliberately spite her parents,' she paused thoughtfully, 'he was devastated. Absolutely devastated when she went away. You should have seen how thrilled and happy he was when she came back, couldn't stop grinning, he was like the Cheshire Cat. Then, of course, when she went missing, he was beside himself. For years he kept hoping she would come back. Sad, really sad, but now he seems happy enough. Got married two years ago to a local lass and they've got a six month old baby boy now,' she smiled at the thought of them.

'So, this local lad. Who is he? Does he still live in the village?'

'Oh yes, he owns the garage just up the road. There's a certain irony to the situation, he was always mad for cars and spent hours tinkering away with them. Because he lived in, what her parents called, a "rough part" of the village and went to the local comprehensive, they deemed him unsuitable. But he went on to do an apprenticeship and study mechanics at college and got a job at the small garage up the road. Just the two of them, when the owner retired he gave first offer to Tom, who managed to persuade his bank to lend him the money and here he is, at the age of twenty-seven, running his own business and doing quite well by all accounts. Her parents thought he'd be a deadbeat who would come to nothing and sponge off benefits for the whole of his life.'

'So this Tom, he's nice then?'

'Lovely. Goes that extra mile for you, so kind and caring, does a lot round the village. If ever you need your car fixing, or servicing or an MOT done, he's your man. Fullwood Garage. He changed the name once he bought it so that it has his surname.'

'Great. Well thanks.' Katherine handed the money over to Betty. 'I shall bear that in mind.'

'No problem. Have a nice evening.'

'You too, thanks. Bye.' Katherine hurried out to her car to get out of the rain as quickly as possible and mulled over what she'd just been told. Had this Tom person had anything to do with Cecilia's death? Was she really pregnant? Could he have been furious that she had had an abortion and in the heat of the moment killed her? Was Wynenden Farmhouse their secret meeting place? As if by some telepathic sense that she had acquired something relevant to the case, she arrived home to see DI Allix pull up near her house.

'Hello,' he called pleasantly, pulling the collar of his raincoat up round his neck to stop the torrential rain going down inside it.

'Hi,' she replied, racing up to the front door to open it as quickly as possible. 'Come in,' she called breathlessly. She shook her coat off and wiped the damp hair away from her face. 'Yuck! It's horrible out there tonight.'

'Not very pleasant, I must agree,' replied DI Allix removing his soaking coat hanging it over the banister, where Katherine had indicated that he should do so.

'I don't know about you, but I'm in desperate need of a cup of tea. Would you like one?'

'Thanks. That would be most welcome.'

They made idle chit chat about the weather whilst she made the tea, then took it through to the sitting room. She switched on a couple of lamps and drew the curtains to block out the miserable night. 'So,' she said once settled, 'what can I do for you?'

'I just wanted to let you know that your builders will be able to get back on site towards the end of the week, hopefully Thursday.'

Katherine's face lit up. 'Really? That's great!' She paused for a moment then asked. 'But you could have told me that over the telephone and saved yourself a soaking. Was there something else?'

He smiled. 'You're right, I could have done so, but I wanted to speak to you to find out if you had heard anything. I gather that you have had a visit from Mr & Mrs Stillingfleet?'

'Mmm, yes I did. Did they tell you?' He shook his head. 'Well I don't know who told you, but they did visit me. A week last Sunday. I couldn't really help them. They wanted to know if I'd found anything else.'

'Anything else?' he frowned, 'like what?'

She shrugged. 'That's it. I don't really know, Rupert Stillingfleet was most insistent, but wouldn't say what it was I was supposed to have found. Audrey Stillingfleet did mention a necklace, but I got the feeling that that wasn't what Rupert was referring to. You haven't found a necklace have you? She said it was gold with a gold butterfly on it. I think she said she had mentioned it to the police, but I'm not sure.'

'No. Nothing like that has been found and we've given the house a good going over. Your builders couldn't have taken it could they?'

She shook her head. 'No. I was there when she was found. There was no way that either of them could have taken a necklace, even if they had the inclination to do so. We all left at the same time and that was after we had made sure all the other builders had left the house.'

He looked thoughtful. 'Okay, well we're there for a couple more days to go over the site yet again. I wonder what was so special about the necklace that they would come and ask you?'

'Something about it being a sixteenth birthday present, but I really don't think that was what Rupert was getting at. I just don't know what he wanted?'

'OK. Well, if you have any other visits, or come across any other information which you think would be of use, please do let me know.'

'Mmm,' Katherine hesitated not sure whether to pass on what Betty had just told her. He looked at her questioningly. 'I. Well ... I was just chatting to the woman who works in the shop. I don't like to gossip...' She felt guilty about deliberately doing so in the shop. 'But Betty asked me if I knew anything, which I don't. And I asked her if she knew anything,' she flushed in embarrassment, 'um, and she told me about Cecilia's boyfriend. Tom.'

He nodded encouragingly. 'Tom Fullwood.'

'Yes, that's him.'

'Yes, poor lad was distraught when she went missing. Phoned us regularly to see what we were doing about finding her, did that for years. Eventually, I think he realized it was time to move on.'

She felt relief that he knew about Tom and that she wasn't entering totally unchartered territories. 'Well apparently, they were inseparable. But what Betty said, and I think this is pure speculation and gossip but her parents will know, is that Cecilia was pregnant and was sent away to have an abortion and to keep her apart from Tom. Now whether that's true or not I don't know. If she was pregnant maybe Tom didn't know about it. And if he did, how did he feel about having his baby aborted? Apparently when she returned, he was over the moon that she was back, though I guess her parents wouldn't have been keen on them starting up where they had left off?'

'Hmm. Interesting. I knew she had gone to France and the relatives she stayed with were contacted, but if she were pregnant and she was made to have an abortion that could be relevant.'

'I hope I haven't made things worse for her parents. I don't want to distress them any further, particularly if it is pure speculation and gossip.'

'Don't worry. This information will be handled sensitively and ultimately, at the end of the day, they want whoever murdered their daughter to be found and brought to justice.' He rose to go. 'Thanks for your help and the tea.' He shrugged himself into his still soggy coat and disappeared off into the wet evening.

Hurrah! thought Katherine hurrying to the phone to call Dougie. 'Dougie? It's Katherine.'

'Hi, how are you? Any news?'

'Yup. I just had DI Allix here. You should be able to be back on site by Thursday.'

'Great! Thank goodness for that. I've found someone to stay on site overnight for the next few weeks. I've got a mate who's just been made redundant from his warehouse job, not good timing with Christmas approaching. Anyway, he's got a caravan and two big dogs - Alsatians - for £50 a night he's going to turn up at 4 p.m. before we go and stay until we get there at 7.30/8 a.m. I hope that's OK? I know we discussed getting some kind of security in, but it's so expensive. I know you want to keep costs down and I can trust him. He's a great big burly man, so combine that with his two dogs and I think it should put people off!'

'That's fine, thanks for arranging it. I think it's just one of those things I'm going to have to grin and bear. Not really fair though,' she moaned, 'after all, I didn't ask for a body to be found there.'

'I understand. But apart from anything, with those roof tiles worth thousands, they're a prime target for someone to steal and though I've got insurance, it would be a real problem to have to source such a huge number of old Kent Peg Tiles. It could potentially cause a major delay on the build.'

'Yeah, I know. Still, hopefully it won't be for too long. Once the novelty factor for the ghoulish day trippers has gone and the roof is on and firmly fixed, then maybe it won't be necessary to have someone on site every night?'

Doubtful about this, Dougie thought it wise to say nothing. 'So we'll be on site bright and early on Thursday, unless you hear otherwise and let me know. And whilst this mild weather is still around, I'll see if I can get the lads to work over the weekend. Get the foundations and brickwork done for the Garden Room before the frosts start coming in.'

'That'd be great! I'll come down on Saturday then and have a look. See you then. Bye.'

Chapter Ten

True to his word, the police confirmed on Wednesday afternoon that the builders could resume work the following day. Delighted, Katherine eagerly awaited for Saturday morning to arrive, so that she could head over and have a look around her farmhouse. The weather was on their side as it remained dry and above freezing at night, no ground frost and with the forecast predicting the same for at least the next ten days - unusual for November.

Excitedly, she got to the farmhouse for eight o'clock, eager to see what had been done in two days. 'Hi!' she called out as she entered the house, which was already filled with a cacophony of noise.

'Hi Kitty. You need one of these.' He tapped his hard hat and pointed to one sitting on the window sill waiting for her, it was bright pink. 'Thought you might like your own and you know that none of the lads are going to wear that!' he laughed.

How stereotypical she thought, couldn't have bought a red one, but she smiled, he was right, none of the others would dare to wear it.

'Where do you want to start?' he asked.

She glanced nervously towards the room where Cecilia had been discovered. 'I suppose in there. May as well get it over and done with.' She followed him in.

'Mind yourself,' he said indicating to where floorboards had been taken up.

'Wow!' For some reason, despite her logic that the police would have opened up the fireplace, she expected the fireplace to be as it was when she last saw it, bricked up with a small gap. Instead she saw in front of her a magnificent inglenook fireplace with a huge thick oak Bressemer beam above it. 'That's amazing! What a fantastic fireplace!'

'It is isn't it. If we get the beam sandblasted to get all the rubbish off it, it'll look really good.'

'Mmm, certainly will.' She sighed, envisioning the poor girl being stuffed in there and bricked up. What had pre-empted it? Why had she had the life so cruelly taken out of her? Had she died in this room? Or had she been dragged in here?'

'Try not to think about it too much,' said Dougie gently, reading her thoughts.

'I know. I can't help it though, it's so unfair, so unjust, no matter what she was like, she didn't deserve to have her life end that way.'

'No.'

'Any luck with the necklace?'

'Nope. If the police couldn't find it, then it's highly unlikely we will.'

'True. Right, let's get down to business then.' She pulled out the plans and she and Dougie went round the house methodically. The roof was stripped and timbers were being inspected to decide whether they needed replacing or treatment. The foundations had been dug for the Garden Room and the concrete was being poured. Katherine was impressed at how much had been done in such a short period of time.

'Here Dougie, found this when we were digging,' said one of his men, handing over a tightly wrapped plastic bag.

Katherine took it and unwrapped it. Inside was a diary, damp but readable. She looked at Dougie who was thinking the same as she. Was it Cecilia's? Carefully Katherine turned back the cover and there in faded and slightly smudged writing was the name. Cecilia Stillingfleet. Katherine gulped. 'I think perhaps I'd better phone DI Allix,' she said.

'Where exactly did you find this?' asked Dougie. An area where the concrete was being poured was indicated. Inwardly he groaned. Surely this wasn't going to halt the build again?

With the phone call made, Katherine had discovered that DI Allix was already on his way to the house anyway. She couldn't resist having a peak at the diary whilst waiting for him. Her fingerprints were on it anyway, so a few more wouldn't matter, she reasoned, her curiosity getting the better of her. She half expected a grand revelation from the diary, but flicking through it; it seemed like a typical teenager's diary full of scribbled notes and coded words and initials. There were several entries for "extra English!" along with a lot of entries "TF@WF", with a jolt she realized that could be Tom Fullwood at Wynenden Farm. Were they using her farmhouse for secret liaisons? And if so, did anyone else know? She went to the end of the diary and worked back to where her last entry had been made. All it simply said was "Payday!". What she meant by that was anybody's guess, thought Katherine. Suddenly remembering about France, she flicked back. Just as she had found the first entry for her mysterious trip away, DI Allix startled her.

'Hello,' he said.

Guiltily she looked up. 'Oh, hello, that was quick.'

'I was on my way anyway,' he glanced down at the diary in her hands.

She blushed. 'I have to confess, I did have a peek, sorry. I suppose I shouldn't have.'

He smiled back at her. 'No harm done on this occasion. But if there is a next time, please leave well alone for us to deal with. Did you come across anything of interest?'

'I don't know. Inner angst of a teenage girl. I didn't really see much. I was just going to read about her visit to France or whatever it was.'

'Ahh.'

She looked at him questioningly. 'Or was it not a trip to France? Did you speak to her parents?'

'Yes and yes.'

'Sorry. I suppose I shouldn't ask questions and you can't tell me anything anyway, I'm sure.'

He smiled. 'Don't keep apologizing, there's no need. I did speak to her parents and they confirm that the plan was for Cecilia to have an abortion and stay with relatives in France, to try and help her forget about Tom, or as they put it to "get over her silly infatuation with him".'

'Oh.'

'I'm sure you can keep this to yourself though, there's enough gossip going around. The Stillingfleet's have enough to cope with at the moment, without fuel being added to the fire.'

'Of course. My lips are sealed. Oh no!' she groaned.

'What is it, Mrs Muier?' he looked quizzically at her.

'Andrew Battle, that's what and please call me Katherine, Mrs Muier is too formal and always reminds me of my ex-husband,' she paused, 'long story, very boring,' she added.

'And Andrew Battle?' He turned round to see the aforementioned opening the door of his new Range Rover, at that split second he glanced up, realized it was DI Allix, hastily got back into his car and roared off up the lane.

'Now, why would he do that?' said Katherine puzzled.

'I think I may have put him off,' grinned DI Allix.

'Thank goodness! But why would you have put him off?'

'Let's just say, he and I have crossed paths many a time over the years, he's one who likes to walk a fine line with his business interests.'

'That doesn't surprise me, not after what I've heard.'

'Really?'

'Oh, I'm sure it's nothing you've not heard before, particularly if you've had dealings with him.'

'Why was he here anyway?'

'It certainly wasn't planned. I suspect he was coming to hassle me again,' she sighed.

'What's he been hassling you about?' His eyes had narrowed and brow was furrowed.

'Oh, he wants to buy this place. Sir Geoffrey refused to sell it to him despite his persistence over the years, apparently Sir Geoffrey can't stand him. In fact, I had to agree never to sell this house to him, as a condition of my being allowed to buy this house. I don't know what's gone on with them but there's no love lost there. Anyway, Andrew keeps turning up like a bad penny. Keeps upping his offer. I'll never sell to him, even if I hadn't agreed that I wouldn't, I never would. He's such a horrible man. He makes my skin crawl every time I see him and I've got no idea why he's so desperate to get his hands on this place. By all accounts he's got enough money to buy whatever he likes, he doesn't need to rely on doing up houses and selling them on to make money any more. It's a real mystery.'

'Well, if he's being a nuisance, I could always pull him in for a little chat.' Something DI Alix felt he would secretly enjoy.

'Oh no! I don't want him to get into any trouble because of me. I just want him to leave me alone.'

'OK. But if he doesn't get the message, give me a call and I will have a quiet word with him.'

'Thanks.' As though reading his mind, she thought that DI Allix would like a legitimate reason to pull Andrew in for questioning. 'Anyway, would you like to see where this was found?'

'Yes please.'

They walked round the side of the house to the back where the Garden Room was being built and would eventually be attached to the main house. Dougie had halted work on the area and sent the lads off to do some clearing in the main house itself. After much deliberation DI Allix gave them the all clear to continue with the work on the Garden Room.

'Really? I thought you'd probably want forensics out again' said Katherine.

'I don't think so, they've gone over this place several times with a fine tooth-comb. Unless we physically dig up every inch of the five acres and take every single tile and brick down from the house, I don't think we'd find any more evidence than we have and we don't have the resources to spend more time here. If she used this place regularly as a meeting place, she perhaps thought it safer to bury her diary in a secret place.'

'Oh, right. OK.'

'I'll get this back to the office,' he said raising the evidence bag with the diary in it.'

Katherine walked him back round to the front of the house and up the drive to where he'd parked his car. She suddenly remembered something. 'When you arrived you said you were on your way here anyway. Why was that? Did you need something?'

'I didn't think there'd be anyone on site today. I wanted to walk round while it was quiet. There's something I can't quite put my finger on…' his voice trailed off.

'Sorry. The builders are working this weekend and I think next weekend, they want to catch up and get as much done before the heavy frosts start coming in and winter descends. Anyway, just so you know, there's someone staying here every night and I think during the day at weekends when the builders aren't working. Hmm, I'll have to check that. Anyway, he's got two big dogs, so you might want to give a little warning if you want to have a wander round, which you are welcome to. I wouldn't want you being attacked by the dogs!'

He laughed. 'Thanks for the warning. I'll remember that. Good idea having someone protecting your property, there are lots of tempting things here for opportunistic thieves, in addition to the inevitable ghouls who will want to poke round the site. Of course, if anything should happen whilst he's guarding the property, even if it seems like nothing, please can you let me know.'

'Of course. I'll get Dougie to pass that on. Bye.'

'Bye.' He slid into his car and reversed deftly out of the drive and headed off in the direction of the village.

Chapter Eleven

All seemed to be slotting into place and running smoothly for Katherine. That was apart from her car which had started to play up and was getting progressively worse. It had taken her half an hour to get it started that morning and the last thing she needed was to repeatedly be late for work, when she wanted to start early to enable her to take Wednesday afternoon's off to keep abreast of the building works. After several attempts it started that Monday afternoon after work and she decided to see whether the village garage was as good as she had been told, it would also give her a chance to check out Tom Fullwood.

She pulled into the forecourt of the small, but tidy looking garage. She saw someone in navy overalls bent over the engine of another car and wondered whether it was Tom. She got out and walked over to him. Hearing footsteps, the man glanced up from what he was doing.

'Hello,' she said, taking in the stocky male with bulging biceps straining at the fabric of the overall, who stood in front of her. His eyes were close together and his nose had the slightly wonky appearance of one which had previously been broken. His hands were covered in grease and there were smudges on his face. Despite his hard exterior his deep brown eyes looked soft and kind, she thought.

'Hi, what can I do for you?' he smiled.

'My cars been playing up, being a pain starting up in the mornings.'

'Do you want to pop the bonnet up,' he asked wiping his hands on a greasy rag, which had been hanging out of one of his back pockets.

She did as he asked and watched as he poked and prodded a few things. She had no clue about cars and for all she knew, he could be planning to carry out a load of unnecessary work. But given what others had said about him and his honesty, she hoped that she would not be ripped off, as she had been at the last garage she'd used.

'Shouldn't be too tricky to sort out. When would you like it done?'

'As soon as really, but I work and need the car to get there and back. If it manages to keep going for the rest of the week, how about Saturday?'

'Sure, no problem. Drop it off first thing and I'll get it done during the morning for you. I think you only need a couple of small parts so it shouldn't cost too much, unless I discover something whilst I'm working on it. Do you live locally?'

She hesitated. 'I'm living in Wynenden Close temporarily.'

'Well, if you have any problems starting it this week, give me a bell and I'll nip round and try to get it going for you.'

'Oh, thanks!' she hadn't expected that.

'No problem,' he smiled, 'see you on Saturday.'

'Sure, great, OK. See you then.' Did he not need her name or a phone number? He must be very trusting, she mused, getting back into her car and driving off. Once home she reversed up the small drive, so that if the car did need help starting it was easier to access the engine.

The phone was ringing when she opened the front door. Dropping everything down and slamming the door behind her, she raced to get it before the answer phone kicked in. 'Hello?' she said breathlessly.

'Hello Katherine. Have I caught you at a bad time?' It was Ted.

'Oh no, not at all. I've just got in from work.' She was pleased to hear from him, having wondered how long it would be before he phoned after their drink a couple of weeks previously. She was determined not to chase after him, after all, it had only been a casual drink she reasoned.

'Sorry I haven't phoned earlier, it's very remiss of me. My only excuse is that work has been manic, but then it usually is, so perhaps that's no excuse and I should manage my time more effectively. Thanks for the other night, I had a really good time.'

'Despite Andrew Battle turning up!' she laughed.

He chortled. 'Yes, despite that. Anyway, I wondered if perhaps you'd like to do it again some time?'

'Yes, that'd be nice. Just let me know when you're free.'

He groaned. 'I'm afraid it probably won't be for a couple of weeks, hope that's OK?'

'That's fine, whenever, I know everyone's busy, particularly at this time of year with Christmas parties coming up and all that.'

'I wish! No such luck for me.'

'Oh dear, never mind, they can be rather boring some-times anyway.' She tried to console him, but actually she rather enjoyed socializing and all things festive, in the run up to Christmas.

'You're too kind. Anyway, the other reason I'm ringing is to forewarn you that Sir Geoffrey is going to be heading out to the farmhouse at some point soon. He's been talking about it for a while and is determined to do so.'

'That's fine. He mentioned it when I saw him, I just hope he likes what I'm doing. I know he saw the plans for the Garden Room and the proposed changes, but seeing them in the flesh can be rather different.'

'Don't worry, I think he's just curious. Anyway, I've got to go, pile of paperwork with my name on it waiting for me. I'll call you soon. Take care. Bye.'

'Bye.' She had a warm, fuzzy, feeling as she put the phone down.

When Katherine met with Dougie on the Wednesday to go through the inevitable queries which were cropping up, she mentioned that Sir Geoffrey would be paying a visit to forewarn him. The build was progressing well and she left them to it, promising to return on Saturday to iron out further queries.

Bright and early on the following Saturday, Katherine dropped her car down at Fullwood Garage. Tom was there beavering away, even though it was only 8 a.m. He was accompanied by a young, lanky, spotty, lad who turned out to be helping Tom every Saturday and was mad keen on cars.

'Morning,' she called, retrieving her rucksack out of the back seat.

'Morning,' he smiled, 'what time would you like to pick it up?'

'Um, I don't mind really. Sometime this afternoon?'

'That's fine, I'll have it ready by lunchtime. I normally close about 2 o'clock but I'll be here 'til about 4 o'clock today, so turn up when it suits you.'

'Thanks.'

'You off on a nice walk?' he enquired pleasantly, having observed the walking boots, jeans, thick jumper, waterproof jacket, hat, gloves and rucksack.

'I'm walking up to the house to see what the builders have been up to,' she blurted out before realizing what she'd said.

'Doing a house up are you? Where is it?' he asked good naturedly.

'Um, er, Wynenden Farmhouse,' she stuttered, but observed him keenly, watching for what kind of reaction her words would procure.

He paled slightly. 'Oh. That's a nice house,' he replied woodenly.

'It is,' she paused. 'Look, I'm sorry, I know,' she hesitated, 'about you and Cecilia and I'm sorry.'

'Thanks,' he said quietly. 'You were there when she ...' his voice crackled with emotion, 'when she was found?'

Katherine nodded. 'Sorry.'

He shrugged and gazed into the distance. Katherine thought he had a haunted look about him, ghosts from the past catching up with him.

'It must be difficult for you,' she ventured, 'after so much time. I gather you and she were very close.'

He sighed. 'We were soul mates. We were going to be together forever.'

'It must have been hard for you, trying to be together with her parents so disapproving of your relationship.'

His eyes snapped up and hardened. 'Huh, they didn't truly care about their daughter, she was just some kind of trophy, an accessory to the lifestyle they aspired to. They didn't really know her. I blame them for her death. If they hadn't tried to force her to be someone she wasn't, this would never have happened. If they hadn't sent her away...,' his voice trailed off.

Feeling she'd over stepped the mark, Katherine stood awkwardly and said nothing.

'Anyway,' he suddenly said in a business like manner, 'I'll have the car ready by lunchtime.' He turned and went back to the car he'd been working on.

'Thanks, I'll leave the keys here,' she said placing them on a shelf just inside the garage doors.

She walked briskly for the twenty-five minutes it took to get from the village to the house, mulling over the conversation, barely seeing the beautiful surrounding countryside with the last few richly coloured autumnal leaves fluttering down, the fields bare, preparing for another winter, the hedgerows empty of their summer offerings. By the time she reached the house she was warm and out of breath from the exertion, the walk had reminded her that she needed to get fit and do more exercise, more walks and back to the swimming which she loved, was what was required she concluded.

She was again amazed at how quickly the work was progressing. The roof timbers were up for the Garden Room and they had almost completed replacing the rotten timbers on the main roof. By next week they would be felt and battening both the roof's followed by the tiling. The full height glass windows, which would run from the base of the roof structure in the Garden Room down to the brick work, which was six courses high in reclaimed brick to match, as closely as possible, the original building, had been ordered and the house would then be completely water tight. Excitedly she could see it all coming together, as her builders performed miracles and her evenings spent poring over every detail was coming in to its own. The house was to be re-wired and re-plumbed and most of it would be re-plastered, due to poor repair. She knew exactly where she wanted everything to go, from light switches to radiators and underfloor heating, to taps, the whole lot. This, in turn, made life very easy for Dougie and his team and meant that it was purely problems which cropped up on a daily basis which needed to be resolved and there was no need to constantly chase for details or information. Dougie knew that when it came to ordering the tiles, floorboards, bathroom fittings - absolutely everything - all he needed to do was ask and Katherine had the information ready. There would be no delays on her part. The kitchen was already on order and would be ready in plenty of time for the kitchen to be fitted and finished.

Having gone through the latest batch of problems which needed addressing and which weren't able to be sorted out over the telephone in the last couple of days, Katherine walked from room to room with her paint charts. She stood in each room, trying to imagine what it would be like, what she wanted from the room and matching a colour to go with that vision. Taking into consideration the aspect of the room and the amount of natural light which came in, ensuring that she wasn't making mistakes such as choosing dark, cool, colours for a north facing room with a small window. She scribbled a note of each room and the colour options she had decided on in readiness to give to Dougie who would get sample pots and put the three choices she'd opted for each room up for her contemplation. The only rooms she couldn't address were the attic ones, these could be done once the roof was on and the new windows - for which she had been granted consent - were in. There was going to be one in each gable end and two heritage Velux windows at the back. This gave her an additional two large bedrooms with sloping ceilings and a decent sized shower room. These were in addition to the four double sized bedrooms on the first floor, main bathroom and ensuite bathroom to the master bedroom. She was just finishing up when she glanced out of the window to see Sir Geoffrey and Ted approaching up the drive. She flipped her file shut and went out to greet them.

'Hello!' Katherine called cheerfully.

Ted smiled in delight at seeing her. 'Hi. I thought you weren't here, your car's not here?'

'In the garage I'm afraid, it's being a bit temperamental.'

'Katherine, my dear, how very nice to see you.' The upper class clip of Sir Geoffrey's voice cut across the still air.

'Lovely to see you too,' replied Katherine pleasantly.

'Thought we'd come and see the house. See what you're up to.' She could see his moustache virtually bristle with excitement.

'Great! Come this way.' Nervously she led the way to the front door, offering a silent prayer that he would like what she was doing and not start making things difficult for her, even though he had no legal right to do so. She took them into the hallway and up the stairs, first to explain what was going to change - which wasn't a great deal - then it was downstairs to explain which walls were going to be removed as several, relatively modern, store rooms were to be knocked down to create a bigger kitchen, which would then create an "L" shape into the Garden Room. Finally she took them through to the room which would become the winter sitting room she had decided. She noticed Sir Geoffrey staring intently at the recently exposed fireplace. Ted raised his eyebrows at her questioningly.

'So...,' he cleared his throat, 'is that where the young girl was found then?'

'Yes, it was,' she replied, noticing that his eyes had misted up slightly.

'And she was there? Alone? All by herself was she?'

'Yes. Tragic, absolutely tragic. I'm trying not to think how awful it must have been for her.' She and Ted stood silently whilst Sir Geoffrey gazed, almost trance like, into the fireplace.

Eventually he muttered something imperceptible, then he snapped back to his usual self. 'Right well, jolly good job you're doing. Now where's this Garden Room you keep talking about?'

She led them out through the front door and round to the back of the house where they could see the builders beavering away, she raised her eyebrows at Dougie who was in a deep discussion with one of his men. She explained what they were doing and how it was all going to come together, pointing out where the heritage Velux and gable end windows would be once the main roof was finished and where the Garden Room would join the main house and which area of wall was to be knocked through to allow it to connect to the main house.

'Excellent, excellent. Good to see life being brought back into the old place. One of my favourites this. Used to come down here with my brother. Of course in those days one of the farmers lived in this house and his wife used to make the most magnificent cakes, we'd come down here and she'd feed us up with cake. Wonderful woman. The cook we had up at the house was absolutely dreadful at baking, she couldn't produce anything decent, her fruit cake was enough to break your teeth on.' He chuckled to himself at the memories. 'You found the Well then?' he asked.

'Well? I didn't know there was one.'

'Oh, yes, over there somewhere.' He waved his hand into the distance.'

Overhearing them, Dougie stepped forward. 'Sorry, to butt in. I forgot to tell you Kitty. The police uncovered it during their search. We've covered it over with boards at the moment and staked them into the ground, don't want any accidents with anyone falling down it.'

Oh, right.' She was a bit miffed that he'd forgotten to tell her this. A Well, how exciting! That would make watering her planned vegetable garden easy.

'Right, well, can't stand around here all day,' said Sir Geoffrey briskly. 'Come on Ted, we've got things to do.' He marched off in the direction of the drive trailed by Ted and Katherine.

'Nice to see you,' he whispered to her.

She felt a fuzzy glow inside her. 'Nice to see you too,' she grinned.

'Thank you for the tour Katherine. Jolly kind of you. You're doing a grand job, just grand, look forward to seeing it when it's finished. Good bye.'

Katherine smiled to herself, amused by Sir Geoffrey's lack of awareness, the pure assumption that he would be invited back to see the house when it was finished, but there was no arrogance there. She had a soft spot for both him and his wife, despite their old fashioned ways and mannerisms. Katherine was growing more fond of them the more she saw of them, but couldn't put her finger on why this was.

'See you,' called Ted giving her a big grin as he hopped into his Land Rover, having ensured that Sir Geoffrey was safely ensconced in the passenger seat.

She perched herself on a tree stump once they had left and happily munched her cheese and salad sandwich, relived that she had received Sir Geoffrey's seal of approval, but bemused that it bothered her what he thought of her project. She waited until the builders had finished their lunch break then went through her paint list with Dougie, he wouldn't need it for ages but she in no way wanted to be responsible for any delay on the work, and so in her usual organized manner, was prepared well in advance. With nothing more for her to do she walked back down into the village to collect her car, this time taking in the beauty and peace of her surroundings as she went. She arrived at the garage just after 3 p.m. to find that Tom was busy working on a vintage car, she wasn't quite sure which one as it seemed to be in rather a lot of bits. He pulled himself out from underneath it and brushed himself down.

'All fixed,' he said nodding towards her car, 'nothing major, the bill comes to £125.00.'

Pleasantly surprised by the relatively low cost, she fished her debit card out of her rucksack and slid the card into the machine. While it was going through they made polite small talk, Katherine unwilling to venture into anything more personal after her faux pas this morning. She was just slipping her card back into her rucksack when the deep growl of a car crept up behind and revved ferociously, making her jump.

'Oh, no,' she groaned, seeing the grinning face of Andrew Battle leaning out of the window of his Porsche 911.

'Changed your mind yet?'

'No.'

'Let me know when you do!' He put his foot on the accelerator and raced off in a roar of noise. Katherine winced at the sound.

'Friend of yours?' asked Tom looking at her suspiciously.

'No! Absolutely not!' she retorted indignantly.

'Making a pest of himself as usual then,' Tom rolled his eyes.

'Yes. What do you mean "as usual"?' She was intrigued to know Tom's feelings about Andrew.

He shrugged. 'Oh, he's always up to something or other, hassling someone or other.'

'You sound like you are speaking from personal experience?'

'Not me personally, but he always seemed to be hanging around when Cecilia and I were together in the village. Always making lewd remarks, that sort of thing. People like him get their pleasure, their kicks, out of demeaning other people, seeing them squirm, making them uncomfortable, suppose he's used to getting his own way and will do whatever it takes to get it.'

'And is that what he did with Cecilia or was it you he was getting at?'

'Huh! He wouldn't get to me, I've come across enough people like him. He's come from humble beginnings like me, I know where I've come from and I've worked hard, worked honestly and I'm proud if people know what I've done with my life. Him, he wants to forget, pretend like he always was a big shot, that he didn't grow up on a run-down estate, he's ashamed of his past. Do you know his mum still lives in the house he grew up in, still struggles to pay the bills but does he help? Does he heck! Never sees her, he's washed his hands of his family, he's a disgrace of a human being.'

Very eloquently put, thought Katherine agreeing with him. 'So was it Cecilia he was hassling then?'

'He hassled, and still does hassle, every female. Bit of a womanizer, convinced no female can say no to him and, bizarrely, a lot of woman say yes to him. It's like he has this strange animal magnetism, can't understand it myself, you see sane, intelligent women giving in to him, they must be mad! He's worked his way through many a wife in this parish too, he's got no morals.'

'Really! Gosh!' He was even worse than she had thought he was, ethically and morally bankrupt, by the sounds of it.

'So, watch out. Unless of course you like that sort of thing,' he looked slightly embarrassed by his vehement outburst.

She laughed. 'No, not interested and he's not interested in me, think I must be too old for him! He's interested in my house and he just won't give up. It's starting to become really irritating now.'

'The house? Why does he want that?'

'No idea, not got a clue. Perhaps it's the challenge? Sir Geoffrey refused to sell it to him and he sees that as a slight, don't know, but what I do know is that he won't get it. Anyway, thanks for doing the car.'

'No problem, you shouldn't have any more problems. See you.'

Chapter Twelve

'So, please can you come?' pleaded the voice of her six year old goddaughter Alice. 'I'm an Angel and I even have a speaking part!' She was doing her best to persuade her godmother to come and see her in the Year 1 Nativity Play which they were putting on that week at school on Wednesday afternoon.

Katherine smiled as Alice continued to plead, it was nice to be so wanted. 'What time is it on Wednesday afternoon?'

'2.30 p.m. Mummy will save you a seat so you won't have to get there really early. Does that mean you can come?' she asked excitedly.

'Yes, I would be delighted to come.'

'Yippee! Mummy! Mummy! Katherine's coming! She's going to come!'

Libby came on the phone laughing. 'You've certainly made her day, I don't think I need to go, I'm not as popular as you!'

Katherine laughed back. 'That's only because I get to do the nice things and don't have to be the nagging mother!'

'Oy! Don't be so cheeky! It's in the job description! Nagging is a very important part!' she joked.

'It's lovely to be asked and it's great that happens to be on the one afternoon when I can be available.'

'It won't muck up your meeting with Dougie will it?'

'No, I had a long meeting with him yesterday and if I eat my sandwich in the car on the way back from work I can go straight to the farmhouse, have a quick meeting and then whizz up to the school for the nativity. It will be lovely. You'd think that working in a prep school I'd have seen enough of them, but I never do, never get out of the office to see the plays or performances and besides, it always means so much more when there's a child you're closely associated with in it.'

'Well, thanks, you've really made her day. Fortunately Henry's only got a Carol Service this year otherwise you'd have to clear your diary to come and see him too! So, I'll see you up there. To get a good seat you have to get there so ridiculously early, I'll save you one.'

'Great, look forward to it. Bye.'

And so, after a quick meeting with Dougie and a brief admire of the tiles being put on the roof, she headed off to the Prep School at Wynenden School to watch the much anticipated Nativity. She parked her old Golf in amongst the substantial collection of new four wheel drive cars, the usual motley crew of Range Rovers, Land Rovers, Volvo's and the like along with a couple of Bentley's and a Ferrari, but a healthy sprinkling of what Katherine perceived as 'normal' cars scattered throughout the car park, reflecting the apparent financial and broad range of parents and backgrounds at the school. She was used to it and not in anyway intimidated, the car park at the school where she worked was filled with an almost identical collection. Katherine followed the stream of parents and grandparents down to the hall, took the programme which was offered to her by one of the older Prep School children and searched the throng for her friend, eventually spying her deep in conversation with another mum.

'Hi,' she said softly, not wanting to interrupt the conversation.

'Katherine! Hi!' Libby kissed her on both cheeks and introduced her to the other mum. They chatted pleasantly until the Prep School Headmaster came out and made a little speech about how much hard work had gone into this performance and thanking the parents and grandparents for attending. The lights went down and for the next half an hour they all sat in rapt attention at the small children doing their utmost to perform the Nativity. So small and so sweet, they earnestly performed and were rewarded by deafening clapping from proud parents and grandparents. This was followed by another short speech, from the Prep School Headmaster, congratulating the children and informing the adults that cups of tea and coffee along with cake and mince pies would now be served at the back of the hall.

'They were so sweet!' exclaimed Katherine, 'and Alice was wonderful!'

Libby burst with pride, as did the other parents. 'I know! It is absolutely amazing what they do. The Head of Music and Head of Drama work miracles. It's certainly nothing we experienced at school is it?'

'You're telling me! We were lucky to get even a hint of music or drama, but that's one of the things you shell out so much money for each term.'

'And worth every penny as far as I am concerned.' They edged their way to the back of the hall, caught up in the tidal wave of adults heading in the same direction. Libby handed Katherine a cup of tea and offered her a piece of cake. Finding it difficult to decide between lemon drizzle and chocolate she eventually settled on chocolate and wasn't disappointed. The sponge was soft and moist and the butter cream was rich but not too sweet. Libby had settled on the same and they momentarily lost themselves in the enjoyment of the cake.

'Gosh that was good,' commented Katherine licking her fingers then wiping them with a paper serviette.

'Another advantage of sending the children here,' grinned Libby, 'they really do make the best cakes.'

'Worth every penny of your umpteen thousand pounds a year you spend here then!'

'Oh, look, there's someone you might be interested in,' whispered Libby.

Katherine frowned, surely she wasn't matchmaking?

'Over there, the tall slim man, perfectly cut suit,' she continued in hushed tones.

Katherine glanced over and saw a very convivial looking male in a beautifully cut suit, pristine shirt and silk tie, dark brown hair sprinkled with grey round the edges, cut in a very traditional short style but with a slightly floppy fringe. He was chatting animatedly to some other parents. Got to be a banker or something, she thought.

'He's the Headmaster,' whispered Libby.

'Oh.' Katherine felt slightly crestfallen. 'Must be getting paid too much if he can afford suits like that,' she retorted. 'Hang on, I thought it was the Headmaster who gave the little speeches prior to and after the Nativity?'

'Oh, he's the Headmaster of the Prep School. Over there is Robert Codell the Headmaster of the Senior School who also oversees the Prep School. He's been here for years, I think he must have been here when Cecilia was a pupil, though not as Head. He was appointed Headmaster two years ago, prior to that I think he had been the Deputy Head for about eight years.'

'Hmm, I wonder if he knew her. He must have known of her, but I wonder if he actually taught her?'

'Ooh, he's coming this way. Tell you what I'll introduce you if I get a chance. I've met him a few times, his wife teaches Year 1, she teaches Alice sometimes, she must have been behind the scenes helping today,' she stopped whispering and smiled as he came directly towards them. 'Mr Codell, nice to see you again.'

There was a beat before he replied as he went through his rolodex memory for the correct name. 'Mrs Lumsden. How are you?' he replied pleasantly, a dazzling white smile on his face.

'Very well thank you and you?'

'Very well indeed.'

'This is Katherine, a friend of mine, Katherine Muier. Katherine this is Mr Codell the Senior School Headmaster.'

They shook hands politely and made pleasantries to one another.

'Katherine has just moved into the village,' she continued.

'Oh really, how nice. It is a lovely village, whereabouts are you in the village?'

'I'm just renting somewhere at the moment.'

'She's doing up a farmhouse,' interrupted Libby. 'Perhaps you know it? Wynenden Farmhouse?'

Whilst the smile stayed, the blood seemed to drain out of his face and he coughed in distraction. 'Oh yes. Lovely house I believe, been past it a few times when we've been out for a walk,' he replied tightly.

'Thanks. Yes it is lovely, well hopefully it will be when it's finished, though obviously we've been delayed a bit what with...'

'Ah, yes,' he seemed to have recovered himself, 'unfortunate business that.'

'Did you know her?' asked Katherine.

'She was a pupil here and I did teach her for a while. Shame, great shame, she ended up the way she did. Well, if you will please excuse me, I had better circulate. Nice to meet you,' he nodded at Katherine, gave them another dazzling smile and eased his way towards another group of parents.

Katherine looked at Libby and raised her eyebrows, she did the same back. When he was safely out of earshot, Libby whispered to her friend. 'What did you think of that? Looked like he'd seen a ghost!'

'I know,' whispered Katherine back. 'Wonder what it is?' At that point they were interrupted by an overly excited Alice flinging herself at her mother.

'What did you think?' her bright little eyes looked up in to her mother's, seeking approval.

'I thought you were wonderful! The best Angel ever!' she hugged her daughter tightly to her and kissed the top of her head.

'I thought you were fantastic Alice! It was an absolute delight to watch you, the whole thing was really special, thank you for inviting me.' She stroked her goddaughter's hair and squatted down to hug her, relishing the tender moment.

'Did you really? Wasn't it fun! It was so exciting, but scary too!'

'I don't think you're going to get her to bed on time tonight!' laughed Katherine. It's going to take an age for her to come down from this.

Libby smiled indulgently at her daughter. 'I know, but it's worth it!'

Chapter Thirteen

There was something niggling away at Katherine but she couldn't work out what, just couldn't put her finger on. No matter how hard she tried her brain refused to retrieve what was bothering her. She flicked restlessly between TV channels, her concentration virtually nonexistent, the phone interrupted her musings.

'Hello?' she said absent mindedly.

'Hi Katherine, it's Ted, how are you?'

'Hi!' her focus immediately switching to the caller. 'I'm ok thanks, how about you?'

'I'm fine thanks, my head is finally coming above the parapet and I wondered if you fancied going out for that drink we talked about?'

'I'd like that. When were you thinking of?'

'How about tomorrow night? I know it's short notice again,' his voice sounded hopeful.

'Tomorrow would be great. Where do you suggest? The Grouse & Peacock again?'

'We could do, or there's the Cow & Mistletoe, it's a bit further away, nice though, old like The Grouse & Peacock, log fires and all that.'

'Great, not been there either. What sort of time were you thinking of?'

'If I pick you up about a quarter to eight, would that be OK?'

'I'll be ready. See you tomorrow,' she put the phone down, a little tingling of excitement buzzed through her. Why was it that, even though she was forty-seven, she felt like a teenager, she wondered?

After another frantic day at work Katherine was glad to get home and glad that it was Friday. The end of any term was always manic; there were reports and invoices to get out, paperwork to prepare for the next term and a million and one other things that all needed to be done before school closed the following Thursday for Christmas. Katherine wouldn't be back in the office for three weeks as she was lucky enough to mainly only work term time, unlike some of her colleagues, and the children were off for almost four weeks. But despite her tiredness she was buzzing with excitement at the thought of going out for a drink with Ted again. She flopped down onto the sofa with a cup of tea for half an hour to recuperate and recharge her batteries and flicked on the television for half an hour of "rubbish" as she called it. There were never any programs of substance on at that time of day and sadly those types of programs were in the minority these days anyway, an unsavoury tidal wave of "reality" type programs having washed many interesting dramas and cultural programs out of the way.

With tea and "rubbish" finished, she hopped up and trotted into the kitchen, popping a defrosted shepherds pie she'd made and frozen a couple of weeks previously into the oven. Whilst it was heating up she ran herself a nice hot bath filled with some reviving bubble bath and soaked luxuriously. Eventually she heaved herself out, ritually cleansing her face and moisturizing it while she drip dried under the towel. She slipped into pre-chosen clothes of slim fitting, knee length, chocolate brown coloured fine needlecord skirt, soft cream silk blouse and a sage coloured round neck cashmere cardigan, she settled on a pair of slim, long, rich conker-coloured suede boots with a slight heel. A pair of pearl earrings and a simple gold chain with a gold coffee bean on it and a spray of her favourite Chanel perfume finished the ensemble. She perched in the kitchen and ate her supper carefully so as to ensure it didn't splash her pristine cream blouse.

Prompt as ever, Ted knocked on the door at 7.45 p.m. precisely. As the evenings were cooling down, Katherine wrapped her pale pink cashmere scarf around her and slipped into her trusty navy pea coat. Again the drive to the pub was made up of small talk giving Katherine a sense of déjà vu. The pub turned out to be just as picturesque as the last; lots of beams, wooden floors, couple of open fires roaring away, but was quieter, less a noisy hubbub and more a serene murmur, but that could have been down to the fact that it was not a Saturday night. They had no problem finding a table as the pub was barely a quarter full. Because of the ancient design of the pub there were lots of nooks and crannies and plenty of tables with comfortable chairs or sofas where one could sit and chat without fear of being over heard. Again they chose a table by one of the fires, there was a small cluster consisting of a two seater sofa and a wing chair. Katherine seated herself on the sofa whilst Ted went to the bar to buy their drinks. She thought it was ridiculous that she felt so nervous about Ted potentially sitting next to her on the sofa, but she spread her coat next her anyway to avoid this, inwardly berating herself for being so pathetic.

'So, how was your day?' he asked placing a large glass of white wine in front of her and flopping himself down into the wing chair opposite her.

She relaxed now that the hurdle was over with and chatted about her day, what was going on at the school and asked him about his work and what had been keeping him so busy. The conversation inevitably came round to the farmhouse and she told him excitedly about what the builders had been doing and how well it was all progressing.

'Any news?' he asked sipping his apple juice and sparkling water mix.

'About Cecilia?' He nodded. 'No, nothing, there's no reason why I should be told anything I suppose, best to just let the police get on with their jobs.' She frowned, there was something and she couldn't put her finger on it.

'You look troubled? What is it?' he asked.

'Oh, nothing, I don't know ...' she trailed off. 'There's something I can't put my finger on and I don't know what.'

'Relevant to the case?'

'I think so, but I'm not sure.'

'About someone or something?' he probed.

'Again, I don't know. It's just a feeling.'

'It's not Andy Battle hassling you again is it?'

'No..., though he had apparently been making a nuisance of himself with Cecilia.'

'Really? How do you know that?'

'You remember I took my car into a garage for repairs?' He nodded. 'I took it to Fullwood Garage.'

'Ah,' the penny dropped.

'We got chatting, it kind of slipped out which house I was renovating and he mentioned Cecilia. Apparently Andrew was always hanging around, making lewd comments and that sort of thing. I can't help feeling there's more to it than that. What if he had done something to Cecilia?'

'Like what?'

'I don't know. Threatened her? Attacked her? Sexually assaulted her even.'

'They're pretty serious allegations, I'd be careful who you say this too,' his brow wrinkled. 'I mean I'm not saying I don't think he's capable of any of those things but what I think, and what he is actually like, could be two entirely different things,' he said generously. 'I'm a bit prejudiced against him as he has been quite ruthless in his pursuit of Wynenden Farmhouse.'

'I get that, I'm really just surmising out loud. I don't know how old he is? He must be, what? In his thirties or forties? And she was sixteen when she died, only by a few months, so he must have been maybe ten or twenty years older than her, that's a pretty big difference at such a tender age. Another thing Tom said, was that he seems to think that Andrew has this animal magnetism about him, that women can't resist him, can't see it myself but...,' she shrugged, 'what if he appeared older and sophisticated to Cecilia? What if it ...,' she stopped herself suddenly, she was going to say "if it was his baby she'd been pregnant with" but realized just in time that few people knew about this fact, rumours yes, but fact no.

'What if?' he looked quizzically at her.

'Oh, nothing, just wondering if there'd been something going on between them.'

'I would have thought with all the gossips around, someone would have heard something and besides he's the sort of person who would brag about it.'

'Yes, but not if she were under aged when this was going on. She didn't turn sixteen until she was away. He may be arrogant and full of himself, but he's not stupid, he'd not want to be classed as a sex offender, a paedophile would he?'

'No, I suppose not.' They sat thoughtfully for a minute mulling over their discussion.

The door to the pub burst open followed by a blast of cold air, interrupting their contemplations; a man weaved his way unsteadily to the bar and leaned heavily on it. 'Double whisky please,' he slurred loudly. The barman looked at him for a moment before silently filling the glass. The man slapped a twenty pound note down onto the bar top and without waiting for his change threw the spirit down his throat, slammed the glass down and demanded another. This one he grabbed and staggered over to a chair, dropping himself messily into it.

'You? 'Whas this? You found summing ...' he slurred loudly in the direction of Katherine and Ted from across the room. It was Rupert Stillingfleet.

Katherine shifted uncomfortably in her seat. 'Oh, hello Rupert. Um, how are you?' What a stupid thing to say! I'm a complete moron, she berated herself.

'How d'ya think? My daughter's dead and what you gonna do about it?' he swayed unsteadily in his chair, sloshing his whisky over himself as he did, about ready for a tumble.

'I think, the police are doing all they can,' she replied quietly, aware that they were now the focus of the whole pub, thank goodness it's not full, she thought.

'Thas not, goodenough,' he slurred 'whose gonna bring her back eh? Justanswermethat.'

'Sorry,' she replied meekly unsure of whether Rupert thought she was a policewoman or not.

'Come on, let's find you a nice table to sit at,' Ted got up and firmly took Rupert, who had staggered to his feet by this time, by the elbow and guided him to a quiet table on the far side of the room, as far away from them as was possible.

'He's in a bad way, isn't he?' she whispered to him when he returned.

'Yeah, poor chap. I don't really know him, lots of people gossip about them being stuck up, but they've always been fine with me, hardly ever see them mind you. How do you deal with something like that? Your daughter disappears and ten years later she's found just a few minutes from your house?' He shook his head. 'Awful, a living nightmare I would imagine.'

'Yes. I guess he's using alcohol to numb the pain.' They sat in a glum silence for a while, the evening kind of spoilt for them and being caring people themselves they could empathize with Rupert and the pain he must be feeling. Eventually, they decided to leave and went back to Katherine's house for coffee. Katherine sincerely hoping that he wouldn't take this as an invitation for anything more. They chatted amiably for a while and sometime after midnight Ted left, giving her a gentle kiss on the cheek in farewell.

Knowing that the builders weren't working that weekend Katherine decided to go the village Farmer's Market and then head up to the farmhouse later on. The weather had turned cold and there had been a heavy frost overnight, the whiteness sparkled in the low morning sun. She shivered and pulled the collar of her coat up higher to keep out the north wind which was gently blowing and bringing the temperature to well below freezing. She was glad she'd put on her pale pink cashmere beanie which matched her scarf and had been a present from Libby last Christmas. Huddled figures hurried up towards the village hall and with relief Katherine burst through the doors into the warmth of the building. It was packed. With Christmas rapidly approaching people were out looking for presents which were slightly different, something which couldn't be found in the high street run-of-the-mill shops. Determined to see every stall this time, Katherine queued patiently for her bread as, yet again, it was rapidly selling out and the queue seemed longer than on her previous visit. She then strolled from stall to stall admiring the many different hand made products and chatting to the stall holders. There was one stall selling unusual designs in silver and she bought a pair of earrings for Libby which were made up of intricate fine twists of silver interwoven with small, circular, amethysts. Pleased with her purchase she decided to have a cup of coffee before inspecting the remaining stalls. She joined the queue and studiously avoided looking in the direction of the long table, she purchased her coffee and hurried past, smiling and saying "hello" at speed before she could be stopped. Fortunately for her the long table was full with the usual mélange of people and the smaller tables near them were all full up too. There were a couple of seats free at a table about as far as it was possible to be away from them and she politely asked the two middle aged women sitting there whether it would be alright for her to sit there.

Katherine sat and sipped her coffee and observed the hive of activity which was going on. The hall was full of people; young, old, middle aged and they all seemed to be buying - good news for the stallholders. Of course with Christmas approaching there were a lot of festive products, fabric stockings hand-stitched and ready to be hung up on Christmas Eve, cupcakes with festive toppings such as Father Christmas, snowflakes and reindeers, jars of home-made mincemeat for mince pies, mince pies, Christmas Puddings, holly wreaths. Katherine tried hard not to listen in to the two women's conversation but being in such close proximity, it was tricky not to. Piecing together what was being said in the snatches she'd caught, she came to the conclusion that the woman called Jane was actually the Headmasters' wife at Wynenden School. Jane was saying how busy he was, always the same at the end of term, how tired he was getting, how he needed a break, how he'd been on edge for the last few weeks.

'I can't understand it,' she said, 'he doesn't normally get quite so stressed but for some reason he is.'

'Maybe he just needs a break. He works so hard, he always has done.'

'Yes, I suppose so,' replied Jane doubtfully.

'And there has been the added pressure of having to make time for the police.'

Katherine's ears pricked up. The police?

'Yes, they do seem to have made rather a lot of visits.'

'Natural I suppose, they must want background on the girl. I know they went into all that when she went missing but that was a long time ago and now that it has become a murder enquiry I suppose they are going to want to go through everything again with a fine toothcomb, they must have to build up some kind of fresh profile again and go over what she was doing in the months prior to her death.'

They absolutely had to be talking about Cecilia. Katherine felt compelled to stay and listen but at the same time felt guilty at eaves dropping into their conversation. Still, she reasoned, if it were that private they shouldn't be discussing it in public.

'Add to that,' continued Jane's friend, 'the fact that Robert was her Form Teacher and taught her English, he's the one who is best placed to give them some background on her.'

He taught her! No wonder he went so pale when I mentioned her, thought Katherine. I wonder what his opinion was of her?

'It is a tragedy, poor girl didn't deserve to die like that. Robert always said she was a handful. It was a shame, she was such a bright girl, could have gone far but would get behind in her work, he said.' Jane glanced at Katherine and smiled.

'Do you live in the village?' Jane's friend enquired pleasantly.

Katherine blushed a bright red. 'Well, yes I do um ...' It was time to own up, she'd just seen Betty come through the main hall door and if she didn't say anything then she was sure that Betty would. 'I, er, bought Wynenden Farm.'

The two women looked agog at her for a moment, too nonplussed to say anything.

'You must be Katherine,' said Jane, 'Robert mentioned that he'd met you. You were there weren't you, when she was found?' Katherine nodded. 'How dreadful.'

'Golly!' was all Jane's friend could muster.

'Mmm, it wasn't very pleasant.'

'I hope they catch whoever did it soon. Her poor parents are going out of their minds. I popped in to see them a couple of days ago. Distraught, totally and utterly distraught. Her mother is beside herself.'

'Not nice at all,' added Katherine. 'I didn't know the girl, but it must have been a shock for the whole village.'

'When she went missing no one really paid any attention to her mother who insisted that something was wrong. Cecilia had run off a couple of times before and always returned. Maybe if we had believed Audrey, Cecilia would still be alive?'

'Maybe Jane, but you can't think like that, it won't change anything now and let's face it, if she had not been so wild maybe we would have taken her mother's claim more seriously. You weren't the only one who didn't believe her.'

'I suppose,' Jane looked none too convinced.

Hesitantly Katherine spoke, choosing her words carefully. 'In what way was she "wild"? I keep hearing this about her, but "wild" could mean anything, I'm just curious to know what kind of person she was.'

'Well,' Jane looked thoughtful, 'she was very willful, she did what she wanted to do, she was always plastered in makeup, every morning the teachers would get her to clean it off and yet later on in the day she was covered in it again. She seemed to have no respect for rules. She seemed very forward with members of the opposite sex and on several occasions was brought home by the police for underage drinking and being found in clubs and bars. But there were times when she could be really sweet. A complicated child is how I would describe her.'

'Hmm, seems like she was quite a handful.' And yet to Katherine it was diametrically opposed to what Tom had told her. She glanced at her watch and, feeling that there was nothing further to be gained by continuing to chat and already feeling guilty about gossiping, she decided to have a quick look at the remaining stalls before the market closed. 'Lovely to meet you,' she said picking her cup and saucer up and rising to go.

'You too, Katherine. I'm sure we will see you around the village now that you're here. Robert mentioned you were renting somewhere?'

'Just a little terraced house on the estate. Bye then.'

Replenished with some homemade pumpkin soup she'd purchased from the market, Katherine again wrapped herself up well against the weather and set out for the walk up to the farmhouse. The leaves in the lanes were crisp and crunchy underfoot from the frost which had remained, squirrels scampered around collecting the last few remaining nuts to store away for the long winter ahead. All was peaceful and quiet when she arrived at the house, no builder and now the roof was nearly finished and the remaining tiles locked securely in the house and ghoulish day-trippers had diminished, no Mick with his dogs, they'd be back later on for their overnight shift. His car was still there next to his caravan, but this was a rouse for any passing rogue to believe that people were present at the property - Mick's wife having picked him, and the dogs, up once it was light.

Katherine stood at the head of the drive and enjoyed the silence, the stillness of the moment, the wind gently whispered in the trees, teasing the last few leaves off their branches. It had been a while since she had had the place to herself and slowly she walked around the five acres, admiring how large it all seemed now that they'd been cleared of 30 years' worth of overgrowth. She relished taking in the house from every angle. The roof was nearly finished; the frames were in for the windows at each gable end, plywood temporarily fixed against them until the glazing went in, and the heritage Velux windows too. The roof on the Garden Room had been completed, the four oak posts at each corner of the extension stood resplendent and the frames for the tall, wide windows and French doors were all ready for the glazing which would arrive on Monday, additional support from steels in place which would be hidden from sight by the time the building was completed. Once this was done pointing work to the brickwork on the main house would begin and the Garden Room would be knocked through to the main house, as part of this the store rooms would be knocked down too.

Taking her keys out she let herself into the house. It was silent and eerie; she shivered slightly and forced herself to not think creepy thoughts. Internally little had changed but she still revelled in the opportunity to walk around without the constant banging and crashing of the builders. Finally, she walked into the winter sitting room and stared at the fireplace. Would she always look at it and think of the girl? She hoped that with time she wouldn't, because otherwise how could she live there? She sighed and left, locking the door securely behind her. She took one last look at the Garden Room, admiring the work that had gone into it and strolled back around to the front of the house.

'Argh!' she jumped as she bumped into the 6'2" frame of Andrew Battle. 'Do you have to do that? Sneak up on me,' she snapped, furious that he was on her land again.

He smiled at her lazily, enjoying her discomfort.

'What are you doing here anyway? You're trespassing. Please leave,' she glared at him.

'I just thought I'd have a look round,' he looked amused.

'You can't just "look round", not now, not ever! Now please leave!' She walked briskly up the drive expecting him to follow her, but he didn't move. 'What do you want? Just leave me alone!' she shouted.

He strolled casually towards her. 'You know what I want,' he leaned close to her, entering her personal space, making her squirm and stagger backwards. 'I want this house and I won't stop until I get it,' he'd moved in closer again, she could feel his warm minty breath on her face.

'Are you threatening me?' she stammered.

He smiled at her, each time she shuffled backwards, he leaned in closer to her, his sapphire blue eyes were hard and cold. 'Merely pointing out a fact.'

Something snapped inside her. 'Is this what you do? Go round bullying people until they give in?' He shrugged and grinned at her. 'Is that what you did to Cecilia Still-ingfleet?'

His eyes flashed dangerously. 'Why are you talking about her?' he snapped.

Touched a sore point, thought Katherine, herself so wound up she could barely control her anger. 'What did you do? Force yourself on to her? Not give her any choice?'

He glared at her, then instantly changed, he laughed at her. 'You don't know what you're talking about.'

'Admit it, go on!'

'I didn't have to force myself on to her. She was gagging for it. Couldn't keep away from me. She was a right little goer,' he licked his lips surreptitiously at the memory. 'For someone so young, she sure knew what she was doing.' He glanced at Katherine's shocked face and laughed. 'Jealous are you? Want a piece of me too?' he looked her up and down.

'What?' she exploded. 'You arrogant, self-centered, hateful man. You know what you are? You're a paedophile! You need locking up! She was fifteen! How could you? How could you take advantage of such a young girl? You're sick,' she spat.

'Like I said, she was ripe for the plucking. She pestered me for weeks, on and on she went, raising her skirt length higher, lowering her top, silly tart. Very versatile, as I remember, particularly liked it in the back of my cars. Of course I didn't quite have the collection I've got now, but we certainly made the most of what I did have,' he grinned at her.

She couldn't believe how proud of himself he was, she felt sick to her stomach, bile lurking sourly in the back of her throat, ready to leap out, it took all the power inside her to restrain it. 'Get off my land! Get off it!' she shrieked. 'I'll report you. You won't get away with this.'

He gazed at her for a moment, his eyes piercing into her, then laughed again and walked past her. 'Go ahead,' he replied casually, 'you can't prove it. She's dead!' With that he sauntered arrogantly to his Range Rover and roared off.

Katherine stood there stunned, shaking from the shock. She slowly walked up the drive trying to absorb what he'd told her, in a daze she walked back to her little terrace and let herself in. She leaned against the kitchen sink still wrapped up against the outside chill and gazed unseeingly into the postage stamp sized garden. Eventually she put the kettle on to make some sweet tea to help with the shock, picked the phone up and dialled the police, asking for DI Allix.

Chapter Fourteen

DI Allix turned up accompanied by DS Windsor a couple of hours after receiving Katherine's phone call. DS Windsor, as usual, looked neat, smart, un-crumpled and unruffled by life. Her boss, in comparison, looked slightly creased around the edges and took up Katherine's offer of a cup of coffee, leaving DS Windsor poised and ready with her notebook and pen.

They listened in silence as Katherine recounted what had occurred up at the farmhouse earlier that afternoon, DS Windsor neatly taking notes throughout. When she had finished DI Allix sat there looking thoughtful, she could see his mind whirring. Did he believe her? Did he think she was making it up? She began to doubt herself. Would anyone believe her?

'Well,' he said, finally breaking the silence. 'We'll bring him in for questioning, he's a slippery character who knows his rights. We need some hard evidence to prove it and he knows it. Threatening you is something else we can bring him in on, but again it's your word against his. I know I believe you, but it could be a hard one to prove with no witnesses. Like I said, he knows his rights. If he

141

should behave in this manner again, please let us know immediately.'

Katherine shuddered at the prospect. 'I just hope he doesn't come up to the farmhouse again or maybe I'll just have to make sure I don't go up there alone. But what am I going to do once the work is complete and I've moved in? I can't hide from him for the rest of my life,' she looked pleadingly at the two of them.

'I can but hope that after a warning from us he'll leave you alone, but as I've said, if he doesn't, let us know,' he looked kindly at her.

'Mmm, I hope so. I just can't understand why he's so keen to buy the house. It seems as though he's obsessed. Perhaps you could find out?'

'Whatever his reason, he's not likely to tell us, but I will do a little digging to try to find out.' He rose to go and DS Windsor snapped her notebook shut purposefully. 'I'll keep you posted but I would ask you to keep this information to yourself. Whilst I feel what you are saying is true, it could be hard to prove and I'm sure Cecilia's parents are distressed enough.'

'Yes, of course. I won't tell anyone. I saw Rupert Stillingfleet last night. He was in a bad way, had had far too much to drink.'

'Hmm, where was that?'

'The Cow & Mistletoe.'

'I hope he wasn't driving? It's remote that pub, certainly not within walking distance of his house.'

'I don't know I'm afraid. I left before he did but it looked as though the barman was keeping an eye on him, I suppose he didn't want any trouble in the pub.'

'Right, well I'll be in touch. Thank you for informing us. Good bye.'

'Bye.' She closed the door behind them and heaved a sigh of relief. Checking that the door was locked, she put the chain on as added security, as far as she knew Andrew did not know where she was temporarily living but she wasn't going to take any chances. Feeling drained she reached for the cooking brandy again and poured herself a generous quantity. For a moment she hesitated, remembering Rupert Stillingfleet, she didn't want to become like him and be reliant on alcohol when times were tough. Don't be silly, she told herself, one drink isn't going to hurt, but then perhaps that's what alcoholics told themselves as they started out on their unwitting road to addiction?

Feeling brighter the next day she pottered round, went for a brisk walk around the village - keeping within view of houses in case Andrew should make a sudden appearance - and settled down to spend the afternoon writing Christmas cards. With three weeks to go, other than purchasing the Christmas cards, she had not given it much thought. She synced her phone to her Bose speaker, went on to Spotify, searched for a suitably Christmassy album, selected play and allowed the Christmas music to get her into the mood and busily wrote. Stopping to make a cup of tea, she impulsively picked up the phone and rang Libby.

'Hiya, it's me. How's it going?'

'Hi Kitty, you beat me to it, I was about to call you. You free next Friday morning?'

Katherine did a mental diary check, school would have broken up at lunchtime the day before and she was officially off duty after the staff Christmas lunch began which was once all the children had been safely packed off for the holidays with their parents. 'Yup, thinks so. Why?'

'I'm having coffee with a friend; she's got another friend coming who I think you would be interested to meet.'

'Really? Why?'

'She's got two children; a six year old and a twenty-six year old.'

'Wow, that's a bit of an age gap, but what's that got to do with me?'

'Ah, well, her eldest daughter went to Wynenden School. Not only was she in the same class as Cecilia Stillingfleet, she was her best friend!' Libby sounded triumphant with this piece of news.

'Really? Gosh. Does she know that Cecilia was found at my house?'

'Yes, she's quite keen to meet you apparently. Anyway, if I pick you up about 10 o'clock I'll drive you there,' she paused, 'I feel I ought to warn you that there are going to be half a dozen young children running around.'

'I'll bring my earplugs then!'

'Great! Anyway, how's your weekend been?'

Katherine went on to recount what she had already told the police and managed to persuade Libby that she was fine and that there was no need for her, Katherine, to pack the house up and move in with them until the farmhouse was ready.

'Really, I am absolutely fine, it's OK,' she said sounding braver than she actually felt.

'You sure?' asked Libby suspiciously. 'Are you sure you're not just trying to keep me happy but underneath you're a quivering wreck? What about if I come over and stay for a couple of nights?'

'No, absolutely not! I'm fine and your family needs you. I'll see you on Friday as planned OK?'

'You quite sure? I mean totally 100% sure?'

'Yes! Now buzz off and go and play with your gorgeous children or something and leave me in peace to write my Christmas cards. Bye!' she put the phone down laughing, feeling perked up from her chat.

With the mad final push to the end of the term over with, it was with relief that Katherine awoke on Friday morning safe in the knowledge that the next three weeks were hers; no work, no racing into the office. The Christmas lunch had been fun, all staff having let out a collective sigh of relief that the term had ended and ended well. She was sure it was something to do with the shortened daylight hours of winter which made everyone seem more tired, certainly the children were exhausted and in need of their much needed break.

After a leisurely breakfast, Katherine showered and dressed in readiness for her morning out with Libby and the children. She was intrigued to meet the friend of a friend whose daughter had been best friends with Cecilia, hoping to gain some insight into the girl. Though they had arranged for Katherine to go with Libby in her car, she decided to take her own car and follow Libby, giving her the freedom to go straight up to the farmhouse afterwards and to not hold Libby up if her plans changed. They set off in convoy and fifteen minutes later arrived at a neat, modern, mellow-brick house set in the middle of an acre. Henry and Alice leapt out of the car as soon as the engine had been turned off and banged on Katherine's window, eager to see her. She got out and hugged them both before they raced off up the drive to knock on the door.

The door was opened by a pleasant looking woman with long auburn hair which curled luxuriously around her shoulders, her freckled face was welcoming and she greeted Katherine warmly, ushering both her and Libby in out of the cold. Libby introduced the woman as Marcia.

'Welcome to the mad house! I'm afraid my two were already hyped up with Christmas coming but when I told them this morning that Henry and Alice were coming over and Sammy too, they seemed to disappear into another stratosphere!' They walked past a playroom which was filled with the noise of the children all talking at once. 'I think we'll go and hide in the kitchen, it'll be quieter than the sitting room.' The sitting room being the room adjacent to the playroom.

They walked into a light airy kitchen which opened up into a conservatory creating a large rectangle, kitchen area at one end, dining area in the middle and opening out into the conservatory beyond that. In the conservatory sitting on one of the wicker based sofas was a small plump woman with a very short, severe, blonde hair cut. She rose when she saw the trio and walked over to them smiling shyly.

Marcia introduced Libby and Katherine to Suzie and they politely chatted whilst Marcia busied herself with her Gaggia coffee machine making cappuccino's for them all. She then produced six beakers, some orange juice and some homemade star shaped biscuits with the decorations having most obviously been created by her children. For the adults she popped some mini mince pies onto a plate and they carried their refreshments over to the conservatory and chatted politely as they settled into getting to know one another. After several interruptions from the children, Marcia finally brought up the subject of Cecilia.

'I have to confess that I had forgotten all about Cecilia until news of the discovery of her remains came out,' she said.

'There's no reason why you would have remembered her,' replied Suzie, 'I too had not thought about her for a long time, though Claire had - that's my eldest daughter,' she added for Libby and Katherine's benefit, 'it's distressing to think what that poor girl must have gone through.'

'I know, it's hard to believe that anybody could do such a thing. I mean you read and hear about murders all the time in the media but it doesn't seem as real as when it actually happens so close to home.'

'I think we've become too de-sensitized, it's become so frequent in the news that we don't pay as much attention as perhaps we would have years ago. There doesn't seem the reality that the person who was killed was a real person, someone's wife or daughter, husband, son, mother, father,' added Marcia.

'I hate it. I tend to want to bury my head in the sand, pretend it's not happening, because if I think about it too much I think about my children and what if something like that happened to them? It makes me feel sick and I want to hide them away, which would not be healthy for them.' Libby shivered as she said this; just talking about it gave her the creeps.

'It must have been so shocking for you Katherine, to find her? Libby told me that you had.'

'Horrible. In some ways it didn't seem real, like that sort of thing couldn't happen in a house I owned. I think about her so much, every time I enter the farmhouse I see her and yet I know virtually nothing about her. The local gossips classed her as "wild" but this was the opposite to what her boyfriend told me.'

'You've met Tom?' asked Suzie.

'Yes, as you know he owns the garage in the village and my car was playing up. We started chatting and he eventually told me about her, he said they were made for each other, that they were soul mates.'

'He was a lovely lad, I only met him a couple of times and haven't seen him since. My daughter Claire was Cecilia's best friend, they'd known each other since they started at the Prep School in Reception. They were glued to each other, spent hours talking and doing what teenage girls do. She came to our house a lot, Claire only went to Cecilia's house a half dozen times in the whole of the time that she knew her. Cecilia didn't really get on terribly well with her parents, though from what Claire said she got on better with her mother than her father. I don't think she was terribly happy at home and I know her parents were totally opposed to her relationship with Tom, they saw it as her ruining her life.'

Katherine sipped her second cappuccino her mind popping with questions. 'So, what was she like when she was older, a teenager?'

Suzie blew thoughtfully through her lips. 'Well ..., I suppose I would sum her up as complex. She was, from what Claire told me and my observations, very strong willed, I worried that she might lead Claire astray but she didn't. Some people found her abrupt and obnoxious but she was always very kind, very sweet when she was with us. There was a sort of need about her, almost a desire for her to be a part of our family and she was a really good friend to Claire, you knew that no matter what, she would always be there for her and stand up for her. That's why it was so strange when she disappeared. I know no one believed Cecilia's mother when she said she had gone missing, even her husband, I think, thought that she was over reacting and told the police so too. But she didn't tell Claire where she was going and she *always* did, she'd run off a couple of times but I found out later that she had always told Claire. Mind you, I did give her a telling off for not letting me or her parents know that Cecilia was alright. That's why when she did go missing Claire was so insistent that something was wrong, when I grilled her she swore that she didn't know where Cecilia was and I believed her, of course now we know why,' she looked sadly into her coffee.

'Did, or does, your daughter have any idea as to why Cecilia was killed?' asked Katherine.

'I've asked her and it's something she has asked herself a million times, but there's no reason she could think of. She did say that if it had turned out to be suicide she would have been less surprised.'

'Really? Why's that?'

'Cecilia always had the air of a troubled child but I could never find any reason for it. Claire told me after Cecilia went missing that there had been something going on at the school.'

Libby's ears pricked up at mention of the school where her children were educated. 'What sort of trouble?'

Suzie glanced nervously at Marcia who nodded encouragingly. 'Well, it's rather delicate, I mean I can't prove anything and because I couldn't I didn't take it further at the time. I asked around subtly but back then these things weren't really talked openly about and if it was, it was put down to the child being hysterical. Certainly no one would have believed Cecilia, I struggled when Claire told me but I know with both the girls they may have omitted to tell me the truth sometimes but neither of them out rightly lied to me or my husband, and there is a difference.'

Katherine and Libby held their breath; gripped by what Suzie was saying but both for different reasons, Katherine because she thought it might have some relevance to Cecilia's death and Libby because there was a pit of dread in her stomach, what had happened at the school where she was sending her beloved children too?

Suzie cleared her throat apprehensively. 'Please bear in mind that what I'm about to tell you is in the past, I don't really want it being dragged up and causing trouble,' she glanced at Katherine and Libby who nodded in understanding. 'Cecilia was a bright girl, could have gone far, her parents had high expectations of her, but she didn't always settle down to her studies and got behind, particularly in English.'

Katherine made a sharp intake of breath, stopping Suzie in her tracks. With a jolt Katherine remembered all the entries in Cecilia's diary for "extra English!" They looked questioningly at her. 'Sorry,' she murmured, 'please, go on,' she urged Suzie.

'Because she was behind in her English, it was suggested she have extra English lessons. These she had with the Head of English, who at that time was Mr Codell.'

'What? You mean Robert Codell, the current Headmaster?' squeaked Libby.

'Yes. Um, that's why this is um, er, delicate,' she paused, 'according to Claire, which is what she had been told by Cecilia, he was giving her more than extra English lessons...' her voice trailed off and she blushed.

It took a moment for the penny to drop and when it did they sat stunned and opened mouthed. Libby had gone pale and felt faint and it was Katherine who spoke first.

'Do you mean,' she gulped, 'do you mean that he was abusing her? That he was having sexual intercourse with her?'

Suzie nodded.

'That's awful,' whispered Libby.

'So what did you do when you found out?' asked Katherine.

'I didn't rush in to anything. I was stunned, so shocked, I mean, he taught my daughter English. She assured me that he hadn't done anything to her and that she hadn't heard rumours of a similar thing happening to anyone else. Anyway, my husband and I discussed it and discussed it and eventually we both went to see the then Headmaster. He all but laughed in our faces,' she said bitterly, the memory still vivid.

'What! How could he do that? Surely he had to take your concerns seriously? Weren't there procedures he had to follow?'

'If there were, he wasn't going to follow them. If I'd known before Cecilia disappeared, then maybe we could have spoken to her parents, taken it further, but we didn't, no one knew where she was and without her to back up what Claire had said there was no proof, no evidence. But

I know Claire and, yes, I know that all parents tend to think that their child could never make something of such magnitude like this up, but I knew she wouldn't have. I spoke to her recently about it again, she's twenty-six now - her own person - and she still maintains that that is what was going on. In fact she's now wondering if it had anything to do with Cecilia's disappearance, her death. That's why she said if it had turned out to be suicide she would have been less surprised, but murder? Neither of us can believe it.'

'I think I'd better make some more coffee,' commented Marcia, 'you look like you need it.' She herself was not surprised, Suzie had told her a few days previously and knowing that Libby's friend was there when Cecilia was found, had thought that there may be some use in Katherine and Suzie meeting. It still disgusted her to the bottom of her stomach what Cecilia had allegedly been subjected to, such despicable behaviour.

Libby's mind was racing, there was no way she could let her children stay on at a school where a man like that was in such a position of authority. How could they be sure that Cecilia was the only one? He could have been getting away with it for years and he always seemed so nice, so pleasant and his wife was lovely. But what if she were in on it too? What if they were grooming the younger children? She felt she would explode in distress. Katherine squeezed her friends hand, well aware of what would be going through her mind, she too felt fiercely protective of Henry and Alice.

'So if the Headmaster didn't believe you, what did you do?' asked Katherine.

'We took Claire out of the school immediately and sent her to another one. We couldn't take the risk. It was awful. We thought about going to the police, but who would take the claims of a school girl, particularly one whose friend had gone missing, over that of a well respected teacher with an unblemished record? There was no hard evidence. Believe me, I've worried over the years, I've kept my ears open to gossip and if there had been a hint of it, just a whisper that he may still be doing this, I would have been straight down to the police station.'

'Now we know that Cecilia is dead, it could be relevant, very relevant.'

'I know. I knew I had to go to the police, when Marcia said that it was a friend of a friend of hers who owned the house where Cecilia was found, I thought it would be helpful to meet, I didn't want to go straight to the police. As it was your house, I thought you might know more? Have an inside on the case or at least know who I should speak to?'

'Sure. I really don't know much. The DI in charge seems nice, not scary or anything and seems to take any information given to him seriously, you could speak to him?'

'If you know him, could you speak to him first?' she looked beseechingly at her.

'Well, er, I suppose I could, though I don't know him well, but it's you he'd need to speak to and your daughter, I guess he would want some kind of statement from her. Is she prepared to give one do you know?'

Suzie nodded. 'Absolutely, she wants justice for her friend. She may have gone missing ten years ago but she still feels the loss and feels it afresh now that her body has been found and she most definitely wants Cecilia's killer found. Maybe Mr Codell had nothing to do with it, maybe Cecilia did make it all up – though I would be surprised –

either way it seems that now is the time to take it further, though the thought of it fills me with dread.'

'OK well I'll give him a call this afternoon. If you let me have your phone number, your mobile number and your address he can get in touch with you.'

'Sure. Marcia have you got a piece of paper and a pen?' Marcia brought a pad and a pen along with more coffee.

'But my children go to that school. What am I going to do?' Libby looked close to tears.

'Not rush into anything, that's what you're going to do. The children are off for four weeks, there's a different Headmaster at the Prep school, I don't think you should do anything rash. Talk to James, but don't rush into anything,' said Katherine with more confidence than she felt. 'And don't, whatever you do, go telling any of the other parents, for the time being anyway, ok?' Libby nodded meekly back at her.

Feeling a need to lift the distressed mood, Marcia changed the subject and started to chat about Christmas and asked what everyone's plans were, doing her best to lighten the atmosphere. After a little while, Katherine excused herself as she had a meeting with Dougie at the farmhouse, she thanked Marcia for her hospitality, hugged Libby and reaffirmed to Suzie that she would speak to DI Allix that afternoon, she needed time for it all to sink in, to put her thoughts into a cohesive order and for the shock to start to wear off.

She was just getting into her car when her mobile rang. She could tell from the number on display that it was Dougie. 'Hi Dougie, I'm on my way,' she assumed he was chasing her for their meeting even though she wasn't late.

'Kitty, you need to get here as quickly as possible,' he replied urgently.

'Why?' she frowned.

'The police are on their way, just get here quickly,' the phone went dead.

The police? Alarmed, Katherine jumped into her car and drove off at speed.

Chapter Fifteen

By the time she got to the farmhouse there were both marked and unmarked police cars in the drive. Katherine could see DI Allix talking to Dougie near the front door. She leapt out of the car, her mind frantic, she was on the cusp of saturation point and couldn't take any more. She hurried up the drive only to be stopped by a police constable, irritated Katherine explained who she was but was still blocked, told to wait where she was until confirmation had been received to say that she could proceed.

'For goodness sake!' she exploded 'it's my house, just let me past.'

DI Allix and Dougie heard the commotion and hurried over. Reassuring the police constable that Katherine had a legitimate reason to be there, DI Allix took her towards the house. Dougie looked distressed and the rest of his workmen were sitting in their vans.

'What is it? What's going on?' demanded Katherine, fearful of what she might be told. She looked from one to the other. 'Well?'

DI Allix spoke softly. 'I'm afraid they've found another body.'

Katherine's mouth gaped, this couldn't be happening, it really couldn't! She swayed unsteadily and closed her eyes. Assuming that she was about to faint both Dougie and DI Allix grasped her.

'It's OK,' she said faintly, 'I'm not going to pass out. It's just...'

'I know. It's a shock,' said DI Allix gently.

It's more than that, thought Katherine, so much more, you have no idea. Today had to be one of the worst days of her life. Snapping her eyes wide open she asked, 'Who? Who is it? Do you know?'

DI Allix looked sadly at her. 'It's a baby, it's not a recent death.'

She looked into his eyes and saw reflected her own fears. A baby? Could it be that Cecilia had not had an abortion? Had actually had the baby? But what sort of monster could murder a young girl and then murder her baby? 'Where is it?' she whispered.

'In the house. Forensics are there.'

'But I don't understand, why wasn't it found when they searched before?'

'It was bricked up, there must have been an alcove at some point in one of the store rooms. To look at it you could see no difference, all the walls matched with the same whitewash, when we started knocking the walls down we ...' Dougie trailed off, tears pricking his eyes.

A small moan emitted from Katherine's lips.

'I'm sorry,' said DI Allix simply.

'Where? Where is it?' she asked. Silently he turned and led her through to the back of the house careful to keep a distance and not to interfere with forensics. In amongst the rubble lay a small blue bundle, she froze when she saw it. 'I can't, I can't look at it,' she turned to rush out of the room but not before she had noticed that there was a small gold necklace with a butterfly laying close to the bundle. 'It's hers isn't it?'

DI Allix sighed deeply. 'I can't know for sure until DNA test have been carried out to match the baby to Cecilia but if I were to make an educated guess, I would say yes. The fact that it would appear her necklace was with the baby would give a possible indication that it could be her baby.'

'But who would do such a thing? Who? To murder a young girl, that's, that's ...' she searched for the right words, 'horrific. Wicked. But to murder a baby? How could anyone do that? A poor, innocent baby, not able to defend itself, that person has got to be evil, pure evil.'

DI Allix rubbed his brow, there were moments when he really hated his job and this was one such moment. 'Let me arrange for someone to take you home. I'll come and see you later on.'

Katherine didn't refuse, she felt weak and sick with the pain which was ripping through her. Then, in another wave, she remembered what she had been told that morning. If this was Cecilia's baby, could it be Robert Codell's? What about Andrew Battle? And Tom Fullwood assumed that it was his baby, did he know that the baby had not been aborted? She allowed herself to be propelled out to her car, a police constable was going to drive Katherine's car and stay with her until DI Allix could see her.

'I'll see you later on,' reassured DI Allix.

Katherine nodded. 'I need to speak to you.' He looked questioningly at her. 'I found something out this morning, something I think you ought to know about.'

'Really? What was that?'

'Not here. Not now,' she replied numbly.

'OK, later then.'

In a daze, Katherine was driven home. The police constable persuaded her to lie down and brought her a cup of hot, sweet, tea which Katherine meekly drank. She lay fully clothed on top of her duvet staring at the ceiling unseeingly. Her brain was going into meltdown with the barrage of information which had been thrust her way today. She refused offers of food but acceptingly took another mug of sweet tea. She shivered all over and dragged the half of the duvet from the other side of the bed over her, cocooning herself up, she drifted in and out of consciousness. A bang brought her back to reality, it was dark outside and light was shining up the stairs from downstairs. She sat up disorientated until, like a slap in the face, she remembered. There were soft footsteps on the stairs and the female police constable who had accompanied her home was silhouetted in the door way.

'DI Allix is here to see you,' she said gently.

'OK, I'll be down in a minute.' She watched the woman disappear down the stairs and went into the bathroom. Her hair was all over the place and a grey, haunted, face looked back at her. She splashed her face, brushed her hair and teeth in an attempt to freshen up.

There were quiet voices coming from the sitting room and she could see DI Allix sitting on one of the sofas rubbing his face again in his hands. A second later he saw her and rose.

'Katherine, how are you?' He looked intently at her. To him she had always seemed strong, the sort of person who picked herself up and moved on, but looking at her now he wasn't so sure.

She shrugged in response.   After all, what could she say? She didn't even know herself. She sank down into the sofa opposite DI Allix and took the mug of tea pressed into her hands by the police constable, who in turn then went and sat in the chair to the right of Katherine and got out her notebook and pen.

'The baby has been taken away and I'm afraid the builders won't be able to work until we have finished.'

She sighed, what did it matter what the builders did? Two lives lost, how many more would they find?   'Have you been to see Cecilia's parents?' she asked.

He nodded sadly. 'Yes. They're, well ...' he grappled to find a word which could describe the agony and the pain that Cecilia's parents were going through.

'They must have known about the baby.   Cecilia was around for a few days after she got back from France before she disappeared.'

'They did. Why they didn't tell me I don't know. They had no idea that she had had the baby. They assumed that she had had the abortion and it was all done and forgotten about.   When she turned up on the doorstep with a tiny baby they were stunned. They kept the baby in the house, too ashamed to let Cecilia take it out. It was a boy, by the way. That was why Mrs Stillingfleet was so insistent that something was wrong when she went missing. Cecilia had taken the baby with her, she had no money, not taken her passport, no clothes, no baby clothes or supplies. Mr Stillingfleet maintains that he thought she'd just run off or run away with Mr Fullwood and would be back within a couple of days when they discovered it wasn't as easy as they thought.'

'I don't get how they could fail to mention that she had a baby with her? It's pure stupidity.'

DI Allix didn't say anything though he agreed. 'It would perhaps explain why they have not organized Cecilia's funeral yet, unsure as to whether the baby would be found or whether the baby was elsewhere being brought up, unaware of his start in life.'

'I'd wondered about that. I'd assumed they'd want to lay her to rest as soon as she was released and was surprised when they didn't.'

'You said earlier that there was something you needed to tell me?'

'Yes, it seems even more relevant now, particularly if it is true. Did you get anything out of Andrew Battle by the way?'

'No, he denied everything. Whether he knew about the baby or not I don't know but I will be pulling him in for a chat to ask him, he'll be aware of DNA testing, it might make him talk.'

'And what about Tom? Have you seen him yet? He's going to be devastated, he assumed the baby was his. I got the feeling there was something he wasn't telling me. Maybe he knew that the baby had not been aborted? Maybe they were going to run away together?' she mused.

'I'm going to see him next. Please, tell me what it is you know.'

Katherine sat for a moment, ordering everything into place so as not to miss anything out and then proceeded to tell DI Allix everything she had been told by Suzie. She handed him the piece of paper with her telephone numbers and address on it.

'I wish she'd come to us at the time,' he sighed.

'Hindsight's a great thing, but surely you can see why she didn't come to the police?'

'Hmm,' was all he responded, his brow creased even deeper. 'Well, thank you Katherine, I will most certainly be following this up. In the meantime, as before, if you could keep what you know to yourself it would be appreciated. A statement is being made later to the press about the discovery of the baby but no details will be released. And, rest assured, I will let you know what the outcome is with Mr Codell. I can understand your friends fears but there may be nothing in this, in which case she could be panicking unnecessarily.'

'Thanks. Well, I suppose I will speak to you soon then.' She showed them out, slid down the closed door, slumped on the floor and burst into tears. Too much trauma piling up had opened the floodgates and was intermixed with the mourning of her own loss, for the much wanted baby she'd miscarried.

Chapter Sixteen

After a restless night's sleep Katherine awoke on Saturday morning tired, lethargic and cringingly ashamed of her breakdown the night before, relieved that there had been no one around to witness it. She couldn't believe that she had allowed herself to become so distraught. Yes, the situation was unpleasant but it wasn't her daughter or her grandchild who had been found at the farmhouse. She'd become too emotionally involved and whilst she knew that the draw of the situation prevented her from detaching herself completely, she also knew she had to take a more practical and less emotional view of it. If she remained too emotional about the situation she was afraid that there would shortly come a point where she would find owning the farmhouse untenable and she had to make the conscious decision, despite the discoveries, to keep the dream of her house at the forefront of her mind.

Her immediate instinct was to hide and stay in the house but instead she got up, got dressed straight away, had breakfast and set off to see Tom Fullwood. It wouldn't do any harm to have chat. She was aware of the odd twitching of curtains as she walked down Wynenden Close and she couldn't blame them. With so many comings and goings at her house and the fact that she owned the farm-house where the biggest drama of the village was taking place, she wouldn't have been surprised if people had come out of their houses and out-rightly stared at her. She pushed her chin into the air with determination and marched briskly to the main road, past the post office and stores, the restaurant, the butchers –where she gave the butcher a cheery wave – past the doctors' surgery and vets and finally crossed the road to Fullwood Garage.

The tall lanky lad, of whose name she had not discovered, smiled at her and muttered something to Tom who was bent over the engine of a car. He glanced up at her, the dark circles and bags under his eyes prominent.

'Hello,' he said wiping his hands on a rag, 'car still alright?'

'Yes thanks. No problems with it,' she paused hoping that the lad would make himself busy elsewhere.

Tom looked at her intently, his eyes flicked to the young lad. He reached in his pocket and took some cash out. 'Steve, why don't you walk up to the shop and get some biscuits? Take your time.' Steve opened his mouth to protest then closed it thinking better of it, took the money and headed across the road in the direction from which Katherine had just come.

'You've heard?'

He nodded and let out a deep sigh, his stocky frame seeming to deflate.

'I'm sorry.'

'Thanks.'

'Did you know before Cecilia came back that she had kept the baby?' she asked gently.

He shook his head. 'No. I had no idea. She wrote a couple of times but she never mentioned it. When she came back I asked her why, she said she hadn't wanted to risk her parents finding out. Not that I would have told them. She said it had taken a while to persuade her aunt and uncle, who she was staying with, that she should keep the baby, not have an abortion. They hadn't wanted to go against her parents' wishes but they're staunch Catholics and abortion is against everything they believe in, which is how she managed to persuade them. They sound nice her aunt and uncle, totally different to Cecilia's parents.'

'So when she brought the baby back, what happened?'

His sad eyes looked at her. 'Her parents went ballistic apparently, particularly her father, they wanted to give it up for adoption but Cecilia was having none of it. They refused to allow her to go out with the baby in case anyone saw her. They wanted to get rid of the baby and pretend that nothing had happened, Cecilia would go back to school and everything would carry on as normal.'

'And what did Cecilia think?'

'She hated the idea, she wanted to leave school, stay with the baby. When I first saw him I was so shocked. I couldn't believe it. She had to smuggle him out, though I suspect her mother knew, we met up at Wynenden Farm. She didn't tell me, she just said she needed to see me, so we met where we had often met, there was no one to bother us, to disturb us there. I walked in and there he was,' his face softened at the memory, 'so small, so peaceful, I'd never seen such a tiny baby and the enormity that he was mine, that I was the father, well, it blew me away,' he shook his head as though still amazed.

He's got no idea that he may not have been the father, Katherine thought bitterly to herself, poor man, hoping he never finds out, but fearing he may well do. 'So what was she going to do? If her parents wanted the baby adopted and Cecilia to go back to school, presumably they weren't going to let her stay at home with the baby and support them?'

'No, we were going to go away together. She knew that she could go back to her aunt and uncle, they had been so supportive of her through the late stages of her pregnancy and after he was born, she felt sure that they would help us.'

'When were you going to go?'

'Cecilia said she knew she could get some money, I don't know where from, she assured me that it was OK, and when she had it the three of us would go to France. She said she hoped to have it the next day and she would call the day after and we could go that day or the day after that. But she never called. I waited and waited. When she didn't call I phoned her parents, her mother started haranguing me, accusing me of taking Cecilia and the baby. I was bewildered, I told her I had no idea where Cecilia was which was why I was calling. She'd already been on to the police but when she was finally convinced that I was telling the truth, she called them again and again, she phoned round the village, phoned her friends, no one had seen her. I didn't know what to think, I felt sure she wouldn't have left me, but part of me wondered whether she had gone back to France and would call me when it was safe for me to join her. Over time it ...' his voice trailed off.

'I'm sorry, really I am.'

He shrugged again. 'At least I know now. I know that she didn't leave me, but I hope they find the bastard who did this to her and to our baby,' he spat vehemently.

'I'm sure they will. Have you told the police this?'

'Yes, last night,' he thought wistfully of his wife Tracy and lovingly of their six month old son, grateful for the support she had shown him as ancient history was raked over, distressing for him and uncomfortable for her.

'If there's anything I can do just let me know,' she had no idea what she could do for him that would ease his pain but it seemed like the right thing to say.

He looked up at her with a haunted look in his eyes. 'I'd like to go to the house. On my own if that's ok?'

She understood, the need to be with your loved one, the place where your memories lay. 'Sure, when the police have gone. I'll let Mick, who's keeping an eye on the place when the builders aren't there, know.'

'Thanks.'

She left him deep in thought and wandered off back into the village. Where was Cecilia going to get the money from? Did she tell anyone else about the baby? There seemed to be a lot of contradiction to her. To Tom she was the loyal girlfriend and mother of what, he believed and may well turn out to be, his baby. There was the kind and polite girl Suzie knew. There was the girl who was wilful and wild. Then there was the image of her as a girl who slept around and liked wild sex and, in addition to this, there was the possibility that she was a girl being abused by her teacher. Katherine couldn't get her head round it. How could one person behave in such a different manner to so many different people? Who was the real Cecilia?

And if she had been such a sweet child, what had made her change? It can't surely have been purely down to teenage hormones? Puzzled and confused, Katherine strolled up the green and into the village hall. Surreptitiously she bought her bread, some soup and a cake and was praying that she would be able to slip out of the hall unnoticed, when Betty appeared right in front of her. Her heart sank.

'Kitty! How are you?' Betty looked concerned, in a motherly way, at her.

'Fine thank you. How about you Betty?' replied Katherine with a false brightness.

Before she knew it, Betty was propelling her over to the table where her friends sat. Their eyes lit up at the sight of Katherine and she felt a frisson of irritation. 'Now, you really must come and have a cup of coffee with us,' said Betty patting Katherine's arm. Katherine opened her mouth to protest.

'I'm sorry Betty, but I'm going to have to take Katherine away from you. Important things to talk about.' Katherine felt weak with relief. It was Ted. She turned and grinned at him. 'Now Katherine, we really must finish that discussion, come along,' he said in a businesslike manner directing her away from Betty and her friends who were looking crestfallen, like birds who had been savouring the juicy worm in front of them before devouring it, only to have another bird come swooping in and take it from under their beaks.

'Sorry Betty, thanks for your kind offer,' smiled Katherine as Ted led her away to a table as far away from them as possible. He quickly purchased two coffees and returned before Katherine could be pounced on again.

'Phew! Thanks for that Ted.'

He laughed. 'I know a damsel in distress when I see one.'

She laughed back and saw the warmth in his sparkly blue eyes and the crinkle of his smile lines around his eyes and mouth. 'Well I was certainly that damsel today. I was feeling as though I was about to be thrown to the lions! They mean well, but I really couldn't cope with them today. I know what they're after.'

He nodded. 'I heard on the news this morning. It's unbelievable, so tragic. I'm assuming that the baby was Cecilia's?'

She hesitated. 'They won't know for definite until tests have been done.'

'I feel for her parents, no wonder Rupert's in such a bad state,' he said referring to Rupert's heavy drinking.

'Mmm. Horrific. I suppose I'm going to get another summons from the House then?' she said referring to Wynenden Park.

Ted's brow wrinkled. 'Quite possibly. They're away this weekend so I shouldn't think they even know.'

'Nice quiet weekend for you then?' she looked hopeful.

'Been working this morning and have got a family party tonight in Oxfordshire. Haven't had a chance to catch up with my brother and his family, or my parents, for sometime. It'll be really nice to see them all. My nephew must have grown a lot.'

'I didn't know you had a nephew? How old is he?'

'About 10 months now. I've not seen him for four months so I guess he's changed a lot.'

'Certainly will have, they seem to change every minute at that age. Have you just the one brother?'

'Yup, younger by five years. My parents converted one of the barns on the farm and moved into it. They're only a few minutes away from my brother and his family who are in the farmhouse, they're loving it, playing the doting grandparents.'

'You never been tempted then? Marriage? Children? The whole works?' she was intrigued.

'Tempted, but never found the right woman to make an honest man of me,' he grinned at her. 'What about you?'

'Well, divorced - you know that, children,' she looked wistfully away, it wasn't the right time or place to talk about what happened, she shrugged. 'I've not been blessed.'

He saw the sadness in her and wanted to know more. He found her intriguing, she wasn't needy like some women could be, she was independent, her own woman and he liked that. 'So,' he felt it wise to change the subject 'are you all ready for Christmas? I can't believe it'll be Christmas Eve a week tomorrow.'

'Me either! And no, I'm not in the least bit ready. I'm normally so organized and would have had the cards sent weeks ago, presents all wrapped and cake made too but all I've done is write a few cards! I can't believe how unorganized I am!'

'You have had rather a lot on your plate, so I suppose you can be forgiven,' he joked.

'You're too kind!' she poked him on the arm. 'Anyway, enough about my disorganization. How about you?'

He grinned and held his hands up. 'OK. Guilty. I haven't done any shopping either but I have written my cards, was posting them this morning in fact.'

She rolled her eyes at him. 'Hypocrite!' she laughed.

'Reluctantly, I've got to go. I've got to be in Oxfordshire by mid afternoon at the latest. If I'm not, my brother is going to be on the war path, surprise birthday party for my mother.' He rose to go. 'Shall I escort you safely off the premises?'

She grinned up at him. 'Thanks, I think I need protecting.'

'What have you got planned for the rest of the weekend then?'

'Not sure, I ought to go shopping but I don't think I can face the crowds, so I'll leave it until Monday or Tuesday. Other than that, not a lot, I might go to the Carol service in the Church tomorrow afternoon, get in the festive spirit and all that, after all it is about the birth of Jesus.'

'Very virtuous, enjoy it and catch up with you next week I hope?' he looked questioningly at her.

'I hope so. I'm sure I could squeeze you in amongst all the Christmas shopping I have to do!'

'You're too kind,' he joked back. 'Well, take care,' he hesitated, tempted to kiss her.

She saw his hesitation, paused and then murmured. 'You take care too, enjoy the party. Bye.'

He stood staring after her, then slid into the seat of his Land Rover, waved as he drove off and focused on the many tasks he needed to complete before leaving for Oxfordshire.

Katherine hummed Christmas carol's to herself as she strolled home, glad of the welcome diversion. She was still humming, whilst she heated up the soup she'd purchased for lunch at the market, when the phone rang.

'Hello?'

'Hello?' stuttered a female voice, 'is that Katherine? Katherine Muier?'

Instantly on her guard, Katherine cautiously said, 'speaking.'

'It's Audrey, Audrey Stillingfleet.'

Flummoxed that Audrey should be phoning her and mystified as to how she had got hold of her telephone number, she hesitated before focusing. 'Oh, hello Audrey. I'm so sorry. Really sorry.'

A sob emitted from down the line. 'Thank you.'

'I can't imagine what you and your husband are going through,' she continued simply.

Audrey sniffed. 'Thanks. I wonder. I know you must be busy. But I wondered if you could possibly come here, to the house? I'd really like to speak to you and I can't face going out, can't face anyone.'

Taken aback, Katherine was perplexed, after all what on earth could she say that would help Audrey?

'Please,' Audrey's voice was plaintive down the phone.

'Um, OK. I suppose so, but I don't know what I can do to help? I don't know anything.'

'Thank you. Could you come this afternoon? Any time.'

'Er, yes, I suppose so,' she glanced at the clock, it was 1 p.m. 'what about 3 o'clock?'

'That would be perfect, thank you. Do you know where we are?' She gave Katherine directions and called off.

Katherine looked dubiously at the phone then went back to stirring her soup.

Chapter Seventeen

3 p.m. found Katherine pressing the buzzer to the intercom at the gates of Audrey and Rupert's house. They were grand and slightly over the top wrought iron gates, some would call them pretentious, given that what lay beyond them was not a stately home but a mediocre modern 5 bedroom red bricked house set in an acre and a half of garden. The intercom stuttered into life and the gates slowly swung open. Katherine got back into her car, for she had driven as the house was on the periphery of the village boundary and she wasn't entirely sure just how far out of the centre of the village it was. In fact, she could have walked it in about thirty minutes and part of her wished that she had, it had turned into a glorious afternoon with the sun shining brightly and the blue sky clear and crisp.

Audrey was waiting on the doorstep for her, dressed in a short denim skirt, with sky high red heels and a low fronted cream wool jumper fitting snugly over her ample bosom and plastered in make-up. Despite the effort Audrey appeared to have made, Katherine could still see behind the mask of makeup, her eyes were red and puffy and her nose looked raw.

'Thank you for coming,' she said, ushering Katherine in.

Katherine smiled and followed Audrey as she click clacked her way across the marble entrance hall to the kitchen. Everything was white and pristine, nothing was out of place and there was no clutter anywhere to be seen. The kitchen too was all white, bar the stainless steel work surfaces on top of the glossy white contemporary units.

'Can I get you something to drink? Tea, something stronger?'

'A cup of tea would be nice please,' she replied politely. From what little she had seen of the house so far there seemed to be no indication that Cecilia had ever lived there, no cutely painted pictures from her younger years stuck up on the wall, no height marks made on a door frame, no photos that Katherine could see. She waited awkwardly whilst Audrey made the tea who got out a tray and laid it with fine bone china cups and saucers, a teapot, a jug of milk, sugar cubes in a matching bowl with tongs, a couple of side plates and a few slices of stollen. When she'd finished the ritual she led Katherine into the sitting room, this too was all white, white walls, white carpet, white upholstery. Nervously Katherine took her cup of tea, terrified that she would spill it and make a mark on something. How on earth had they coped with a teenager in the house? What sort of a life would a teenager have had if she had not been able to make a mess? There were a few precious ornaments dotted around and one photograph of a girl who, Katherine assumed, was Cecilia.

Audrey saw her looking at it. 'That's her, my gorgeous Cecilia,' her voice cracked. 'That was taken about a year before she... she...,' sobbing she continued, 'before she died, before it all started going wrong,' she finished.

The girl looked bright and happy, long, straight, blond hair, green eyes and freckles, a big smile, she looked carefree. How could things have changed so much? What had happened to set the wheels in motion for this tragedy to unfold? Katherine looked at Audrey who was doing her best to recover her composure and sipped her tea quietly.

'She was always such a lovely, happy child and then she started to change. I put it down to hormones at first but it just got worse, she constantly fought with her father, she was rude, abusive even, ran off. I couldn't understand where my precious little girl had gone to?' Audrey looked bewildered.

'I'm so sorry,' again Katherine wondered why she was here.

Audrey blew her nose on her handkerchief. 'Maybe we neglected her? The cleaning business was getting busier and busier and we spent more and more time there, we wanted to make it grow, make money so that we could provide Cecilia with a comfortable start in life, one where she didn't have to get into debt to go to University, buy a car for her, help her to buy a little cottage somewhere. Maybe if I'd spent more time with her, she wouldn't have changed so much. But we were doing it for her, to pay for the school fees, give her the best start in life.'

'I'm sure she knew you were doing your best for her,' Katherine hoped a few kind words would bring a little comfort, after all nothing she could say or do would bring Audrey's daughter back.

'Tell me a little bit about her, before she went to France,' she said diplomatically, 'and what happened when she came back?'

Audrey's eyes drifted off to another place as she remembered. 'She had this boyfriend, Tom, they'd been together for a few months, he seemed nice enough but Rupert didn't want her seeing him. He was convinced that Tom would lead her astray, keep her from her studies, she had to focus, he told her, get good qualifications, work hard, she shouldn't have a boyfriend at her age, he told her. They fought and fought. I didn't see the problem, I thought if they were left alone, let the relationship run its course, it would all blow over. I tried to tell Rupert that the more he made of it, the more she would dig her heels in and that's precisely what happened. Then she became pregnant, just a short time before she was due to turn sixteen. Rupert wanted to report Tom to the police, for having sex with a minor, but somehow Cecilia persuaded him otherwise. She stubbornly said she was going to keep the baby, that she and Tom were going to bring it up together, he was only just sixteen, what hope had they got? Of course Rupert went ballistic, he arranged for her to go to a clinic and to stay with his sister and her husband in France, let things die down a bit, get a bit of space between Cecilia and Tom. He was sure that when she came back she would have forgotten all about him. I had my doubts but went along with it. I just wanted her to be happy and did feel that if there was some distance between her and her father things would calm down a bit, let Rupert calm down and give Cecilia a change of scenery, with a bit of TLC from her aunt and uncle I thought there might be a chance she would revert back to being her old self.'

'So what happened when she returned with the baby?'

'I was shocked, but a part of me was delighted, there was my grandson, how could any mother not feel something for their grandchild? He was gorgeous, absolutely gorgeous. So small, so sweet, hardly cried, I fell instantly in love with him and Cecilia was so good with him, took total care, fed him, bathed him, there was a maturity about her which was astounding for her years. Rupert, on the other hand, wanted nothing to do with him, he wanted the baby put up for adoption. Cecilia begged and pleaded, I begged and pleaded but he wasn't going to shift his view. I didn't know what rights Cecilia had, or Tom for that matter, I just hoped that the baby could not be adopted without Cecilia and Tom's permission, that there would be nothing Rupert could do.'

'It must have been very tricky for you, being pulled between the two people you love.'

'It wasn't pleasant but Cecilia was my daughter and as a mother I would do anything to protect her, if I had to choose between my husband and my daughter, there would be no contest.'

It just goes to show, thought Katherine, that you should never make assumptions or judgements about people. From what everyone else had said, Audrey and Rupert put themselves first before their daughter and treated her like a trophy. Audrey was painting a totally different picture. Even if Cecilia had had the love and support from her mother and some kind of love from her father, albeit in a very Neanderthal way, what had changed? What had made her rebel? A thought popped into her head, had the change coincided with Cecilia starting her extra English lessons?

Had abuse changed her? At that moment Katherine could think of no sensitive way to bring it up.

'What happened on the last day that you saw her?' asked Katherine gently.

Audrey sniffed and wiped her eyes. 'Rupert had banned Cecilia from taking the baby out in public, he didn't want anyone to know. Cecilia was desperate to see Tom, to show him the baby but it wasn't wise for Tom to come to the house. The day before she went missing I'd let her sneak off with the baby to see Tom, they met up at your farmhouse. She wasn't out for too long, didn't want to run the risk of Rupert finding out. Anyway, that was fine, Rupert was none the wiser. The next day, Rupert said he had meetings all day and would be back late, Cecilia asked if she could take the baby out again, I agreed as long as she steered clear of the village and public places, she gave the impression that she was going back to the farmhouse and I assumed that she was therefore meeting Tom. She went out in the morning and said she would be back by early afternoon. She took the baby in one of those papoose things and plenty of nappies, clothes, a blanket and water and a snack for herself, so she was well prepared and she was feeding the baby herself so there was no problem about bottles or feeding him. When she hadn't come home by mid afternoon I started to feel cross. Cross that she had let me down, she'd promised she'd be back by mid afternoon. By late afternoon I was starting to get worried and by early evening I was frantic. I tried to phone Tom but couldn't get hold of him. Rupert came back late, must have been about 10 o'clock, but by then I had phoned the police. They arrived shortly after he got back. He told me not to tell them about the baby, I didn't know why. He then persuaded them that it was not unusual for Cecilia to run off, they were very kind but you could see them thinking that I was some kind of over protective, hysterical, mother. But I knew Cecilia wouldn't keep the baby out, the evenings were chilling down and she adored him, she took such care of him, I just *knew* that she wouldn't do anything to put his health or safety in jeopardy. As soon as the police had gone Rupert and I had a massive row, it was horrible, he stormed out and I didn't see him until late the next day. I couldn't sleep, I just couldn't. I phoned round her friends, I asked around the village but no one had seen her. I phoned Tom and vented my frustrations at him, accusing him of keeping her away from home, he denied it, it was when he started to sound worried that I believed him, he said he had not seen her all that day. It was days before the police took me seriously, then the village realized and everyone was out searching fields and woodland and still Rupert wouldn't let me tell anyone about the baby and he threatened Tom, I don't know what he said to him but Tom didn't tell the police either.'

'Surely though with his daughter missing he wouldn't care whether people knew about the baby or not? Just to get his daughter back would have been enough?'

'I know, but he insisted. Kept saying she'd turn up and then the baby could be adopted out. And as time went by it became harder. I mean how could I tell the police months down the line that my daughter had had her tiny baby with her and that they had both gone missing?'

'Hmm,' pondered Katherine.

'I never gave up hope that they would come home, that they were still alive. Every year on her birthday, and on the baby's birthday, I'd make a cake and light candles. I always hoped, always,' tears were streaming down her face.

'And now? What happens now?'

'I don't know. I don't know how I can go on? My baby's gone. If we bury her it's like acknowledging that she's dead, if we don't I can continue to pretend, pretend for the rest of my life that she may still come home.'

I don't think she even knows about the allegations made about Robert Codell. How on earth is she going to cope if they turn out to be true? That the school they worked so hard to pay for was quite possibly responsible for the downfall of her daughter. That her daughter had been abused. Katherine gulped; it would be enough to push anyone over the edge.

'You have Rupert. Can you not support each other through this?'

'Huh! Rupert! All he does is drink. Have you not wondered where he is? He's out, no doubt getting plastered. He started drinking when Cecilia disappeared, not a lot but over time it has got progressively worse and these last few weeks there's barely a moment when he's sober. I've had to go and sort the mess out that he's making at work, fortunately we have a team who are very supportive, but it's getting ridiculous, he turns up at the office half cut, he's making a fool of himself. He drinks from the moment he wakes up until the moment he passes out. I've tried to talk to him about it but he flies off the handle, he won't acknowledge that he has a problem. I don't know what to do? So, as for support. I've got no one. I'm alone and no one to share my pain with.'

No wonder she phoned me, thought Katherine, she's desperate. Katherine could only assume that it was because her daughter and grandchild had been discovered in Katherine's farmhouse that she'd felt there was some kind of connection, a link between the two of them.

'There must be someone you could talk to? A friend perhaps?'

She shook her head. 'No, Rupert's managed to chase them all away and I have buried myself in work and neglected the few friends I did have.'

'What about the vicar? Couldn't he help?' Wasn't that what members of the clergy were supposed to do? Be there in a crisis?'

'Maybe. He did phone and leave a message but I've not got back to him. Maybe I should phone him?' she brightened momentarily.

'What was your grandchild's name?' Katherine realized that the baby had always been referred to as "he" or "baby" rather than by name.

'He didn't have a name. Not that I know of, Cecilia said she wanted to choose one with Tom. I don't know if they did. I suppose I could ask Tom, I never really thought of it which is peculiar.'

'You could,' though Katherine remembered Tom referring to the baby by gender rather than Christian name, 'and if the baby did not have a name maybe you could choose one for him?'

'What a good idea! Yes. You're right. I must speak to Tom and if they'd not chosen a name, then we could choose one.' This small idea gave her a mission, something to think about, something to keep her going.

Katherine rose to go. 'Thank you for the tea and for the cake.'

'Thank you for coming,' she took both Katherine's hands in hers, they felt warm and soft in her own thin, boney and ice cold ones, and looked directly at Katherine. 'Thank you.'

Katherine left still feeling slightly bewildered, trying to discover who Cecilia really was as a person, was proving to be decidedly tricky, there continued to be so many contradictions. It would appear that the driving force behind the desire for the Stillingfleet's to put Cecilia's baby up for adoption was from Rupert and opposed to what Audrey wished. The picture painted by the village was one of them being as bad as each other, whether the passing of time had given a rosy hue to Audrey's as to her view of her relationship with her daughter, was something Katherine was unlikely to find out. Feeling none the wiser Katherine drove home with her mind feeling in a fog, arriving home she decided that it was no good focusing all her efforts on Cecilia and decided to devote the rest of the afternoon, and as much of the evening as was necessary, in completing the writing of her Christmas cards.

Chapter Eighteen

At 3.30 p.m. the next day Katherine slipped into one of her smarter coats, in this case a pale, moss green, velvet one. She wrapped her pale pink cashmere scarf snugly around her neck, did the buttons of the coat up and slipped on a pair of pale pink cashmere gloves which matched her scarf. Satisfied that she looked smart enough, but well defended against the cold, she set off at a brisk pace to the Church for the afternoon Carol Service. Katherine had not been into the Norman towered Church which nestled neatly at the top of the Green adjacent to the village hall. She assumed that, like a lot of Churches, there would be little or no heating and the building would have held onto the frosty weather which the country was being gripped by.

She wasn't sure whether there would be many people in the congregation as when the media talked about the Church of England it always seemed to refer to its dwindling in number of those attending. She was pleasantly surprised therefore to see, maybe not a steady stream but certainly a steady trickle of, cars driving up and parking in the Church car park which was shared with the village hall, and a few who, like her, were going on foot.

She was greeted, firstly, by a blast of hot air as she walked into the Church and then a couple of cheerful faces welcoming her to the Church. She was amazed to see that the Church was at least three quarters full with more following her in and with still ten minutes to go before the start of the service. Katherine tried to sneak to a seat at the back of the Church in order not to be prominent in her presence. However she was guided to a seat at the end of a pew about half way up the aisle. She murmured pleasantries to those immediately next to her then looked around to take in her surroundings. The Church had a large Christmas Tree to the left of the pulpit, it was covered in baubles, tinsel and white lights which twinkled and sparkled in the built-in lights and candle light of the Church. To the right of the pulpit Katherine could see a Nativity scene laid out, she squinted closer at it and realized that Jesus was not in the crib, perhaps they waited for the day itself to put him in there, she pondered. She looked around her and though, in general, the congregation was of the older generation, there was a respectable gathering of all ages, quite a few families with younger children and babies who were making their presence known by their over excited chatter and the frequent "Sshh" emitting from their parents.

Across the aisle and in the front row she saw Sir Geoffrey and Lady Percevall-Sharparrow, she hoped that they wouldn't see her for she knew that if they did she would be grilled on the spot in front of so many strangers and cringed at the thought of what would be excruciatingly embarrassing, that was assuming they had been informed about the discovery of the baby. Katherine had hoped that as they were away for the weekend they would not be back in time for the service. Her eyes continued to stray around the congregation for any familiar faces, she was startled to see Andrew Battle sitting with his arm around an exceedingly young looking woman - different to the one she had seen him with in the Grouse & Peacock - he glanced in her direction, saw her and gave her a lazy smile. Feeling churlish not to, she smiled politely back then studiously studied the service sheet she had been given on the way in.

The organ which had been playing some pleasant music stopped and the vicar appeared in front of them all to welcome them to the Carol Service. Most of the lights were turned off and the magical glow of the candles lit the Church. Lots of carols, several readings, a brief sermon, some prayers and the service was over before she knew it.

Katherine now felt truly in the Christmas spirit, the service had uplifted her and she followed the sea of people flowing towards the door, managing to avoid Andrew and doing her best to keep out of Sir Geoffrey's sight. Tea, mulled wine and mince pies were to be served in the village hall so after a quick shake of the vicar's hand and words of thanks for the service, she wrapped herself up again against the frosty air and strolled down the path towards the village hall. She noticed a small group of people over by a familiar looking car, silhouetted in the dark. As she came parallel to them she was startled to see that it was DI Allix. DS Wilson was beside him and even more startling was the fact that it was Robert Codell he was talking to. His wife Jane was beside him seeming distressed. Though Katherine could not hear what was being said, the back door of DI Allix's car was opened and Robert Codell ushered in. DS Wilson got in on the other side and sat next to him, as DI Allix slide behind the driver's wheel his eyes alighted on Katherine. He held them momentarily in a greeting and then swiftly drove away, leaving Jane Codell standing, bewildered.

Unsure as to whether to go and see how she was, Katherine was saved by Jane's sudden movement, she ran to her car, jumped in and raced off, narrowly missing knocking down a group of elderly ladies who had been cautiously making their way from Church to village hall. Fortunately, it appeared that no one else had noticed Robert being driven off; at least that's one less piece of gossip to go round, for the time being, thought Katherine.

Ensuring that the group of elderly ladies was alright, other than a little flustered, Katherine went ahead of them into the village hall. The bright lights after the darkness outside made her blink momentarily. The hall was filling up and there were people ferrying trays of tea, mulled wine and mince pies around. Gratefully she took a cup of tea and a mince pie and moved towards the edge of the room feeling slightly like a fish out of water. Everyone seemed to know each other and were chatting happily to one another. She normally didn't feel quite so socially inept, but she felt awkward, she could hardly start a conversation with "oh, yes, I own the house where the bodies were found" could she?

She didn't notice a figure slide next to her until there was a slight clearing of a throat. Katherine turned and saw the pale face of Audrey Stillingfleet looking back at her. Surprised to see her as, by her own admission, Audrey had said she was too nervous to venture into the village, she smiled warmly at her.

'Hello Audrey. Did you enjoy the service?' was the inane question Katherine thought of.

'Hello Katherine. It was OK, nice to see the Church so full. Lovely to see children,' she gulped and tears welled up in her eyes.

How hard it must be to see so many happy families, children, parents, grandparents and to know that you will never be part of that exclusive group, thought Katherine about Audrey. Then, like being hit by a bolt of lightning, Katherine realized that it applied to her too, she too would never be a part of that exclusive group, at forty-seven she knew the boat had past her by and not through lack of trying.

'You alright?' Audrey looked anxiously at her. 'You look like you've just had a fright.'

Katherine blinked. 'I'm fine, she stuttered, 'really, I'm fine,' she took control of herself. 'Is Rupert with you?'

Audrey shook her head. 'No. He ...' her voice trailed off.

Probably drunk again, mused Katherine. She became aware that people were looking at them, not in an obvious, out-right sort of way, but surreptitiously Katherine knew they were talking about them, well about Audrey anyway. As if sensing it too, Audrey shifted round so that her back was facing out to the centre of the hall and she was facing Katherine and the wall.

'Don't worry,' whispered Katherine.

'It's the first time I've ventured out to a village event, since, well, you know...' Audrey glanced at Katherine. 'I took your advice yesterday and telephoned the vicar, he was so nice, he came round yesterday evening and we had a long chat, it really helped. It was he who mentioned the Carol Service, so I thought I'd take the plunge, you know, get it over and done with, do it when something joyful is being celebrated.'

'You're very brave. People mean well, I'm sure they all feel for you.'

'I know, it's just hard, I don't want people's sympathy or pity and one moment I want to talk and talk about Cecilia and the baby and the next moment I don't and wonder what they are thinking of me? Hiding the fact that Cecilia had had a baby? That we didn't tell the police? Rupert isn't helping either by being drunk all the time and he's driving whilst drunk, I've begged and pleaded with him not too but he won't listen.'

Katherine squeezed Audrey's hand and felt silly that she had felt so nervous about talking to people when she arrived. She had nothing to hide from and nothing to feel awkward about, it was pathetic, she thought, and poor Audrey was in a living hell. Perspective had been firmly put in its place.

'Everyone is going to have their own opinion and there will be a small number who will criticize and be cruel about you behind your back, but they will be the minority and unfortunately that's life, but they aren't the people who count. For each one of them there will be dozens who are not like that. Maybe they won't be able to understand why you did what you did, but they will empathize with your situation and feel your pain. Putting it off will make it seem bigger, seem worse, when you do start integrating back in to village life, getting it over and done with will help, making that first step. But you've done that already, you've come here, it can't be any harder.'

'You think so?'

'I know so,' said Katherine with confidence. 'I'm sure you will receive many offers of support too, you're not alone.' Even though you may feel it with your husband being so unsupportive she added silently. 'Come on,' she said decisively, 'let's get you a cup of tea and a mince pie.' She took Audrey by the arm, turned her around and marched purposefully towards a young girl who was carrying a tray with cups of tea and a plate of mince pies. 'Here you are,' said Katherine, passing Audrey a cup of tea, swapping her empty cup for a full one and placing a mince pie on the side of each saucer.

It was mere seconds before someone had approached them and was offering Audrey their condolences, a steady flow of people continued and Katherine slipped back into the crowd. She turned and bumped straight into Tom.

'Hello,' he smiled at her, his face even more drawn and tired than the day before. 'This is my wife Tracy,' an exhausted looking young woman shook her hand and smiled. 'And this, is our son Joe,' he took the cute six month old from his wife and kissed and cuddled him, looking immensely proud.

'Pleased to meet you,' replied Katherine to Tracy. 'He is such a sweetheart.' She cooed at the baby who was grinning his little head off, dribbling and burbling.

'Thanks, we think so.'

At that precise moment Katherine caught sight of Sir Geoffrey and Lady Susan out of the corner of her eye, she could see them approaching through the throng. 'I've got to get going,' she excused herself, 'lovely to meet you.' She slipped through the crowd, out into the fresh night air and walked as quickly as her legs would carry her back to her house.

It was a while later that evening when her phone rang and she put the TV on mute before answering. It was Ted. They chatted amiably about their respective weekends, Ted having had a great time with his family, the surprise party being a roaring success.

He cleared his throat. 'Anyway, I'm afraid Sir Geoffrey was just on the phone to me.'

Katherine felt a fizzle of disappointment, she'd thought he'd phoned her because he wanted to, not because he had been instructed to.

'Sir Geoffrey would like to see you. Apparently he tried to catch you this evening but he didn't manage to.'

She felt irritated. Why should she jump whenever he said she had to? She was grateful for being able to purchase the farmhouse but she wasn't going to spend the rest of her life leaping to command every time he demanded it.

Ted felt uncomfortable asking, he liked Katherine and didn't want to have to be the go between. 'Anyway he's asked if you could come up to the house tomorrow morning, as early as possible. I did say I thought you might be rather busy what with Christmas coming,' he added hurriedly.

'Really, I can't do tomorrow morning or even the afternoon, well that's not true, I could if I really wanted to or it was urgent or it was life threatening, but it's not and I don't see what I'm supposed to know that they would be interested in. Why don't they speak to the police?'

'I know, but…' he was stuck between a rock and a hard place.

'Tell him I will be up on Tuesday morning at 10 a.m. but that if I can possibly manage it I will come up later tomorrow afternoon, though it's very unlikely.'

'Thanks.' He knew he'd upset Katherine and he also knew he would get a blasting from Sir Geoffrey for not making sure that Katherine was there first thing tomorrow.

Katherine felt slightly remorseful at having snapped at Ted. 'I don't mean to be grumpy,' she said.

He brightened slightly. 'Don't worry, I thought you were rather restrained, all things considered,' he joked tentatively; he could feel a thaw down the phone. 'I was going to phone you anyway, it's just unfortunate that Sir Geoffrey got to me first. I've only been back half an hour. Do you think you could fit me into your busy schedule for a drink? Coffee even if that's easier?' he was hopeful.

'Ooh, I don't know,' she replied teasingly, 'I'll have to check my diary,' she paused momentarily for effect, 'I could squeeze you in on Tuesday evening, if that works for you?'

'It will!' he replied determinedly.

'Great. Well if you're not at the house when I come up on Tuesday I will pop into the stables to arrange a time.' The stables were where the Estate Office was, once housing twenty horses there were now none and part of the stables had been converted to provide office space outside of the main house.

'Look forward to it. Bye.'

She put the phone down and still felt a bit guilty. She could have gone to see Sir Geoffrey first thing before she went shopping but she didn't want to. Besides, she reasoned, if I get delayed, the later I go shopping the bigger the queues will be.

And she was right, she'd set off early to do a blitz at the Bluewater Shopping Centre and even though she was there for nine o'clock, cars were streaming in and rapidly filling up the parking spaces, by 10 a.m. she knew it would be full.

There weren't a huge number of presents she needed to buy, her parents were dead, she had no husband and no children which just left her with a small number of presents to get for a few friends and, of course, for her godchildren with whom she would be spending Christmas. With the prolific amount of toys which children had these days Katherine did what she always did when it came to buying them presents, she checked with Libby. On the list this year was another doll with accessories for Alice and a specific set of Lego for Henry. To accompany these Katherine spent some time choosing a book for each of them, fortunately both children loved to read which Katherine put down to the fact that their parents loved to read and also read stories to them each night before bed.

The crowds were thronging and were starting to make the Christmas shopping experience unpleasant. Katherine normally shopped at the end of November, when it was close enough to Christmas to feel Christmassy but far enough away to avoid hideous queues. Even purchasing a take away coffee was a mammoth event. Gritting her teeth Katherine continued in a determined manner, gradually ticking off each present one by one. Hungry and grumpy she purchased a sandwich and drink from the Waitrose within John Lewis, along with a pre-prepared luxury fish pie and pre-prepared vegetables for that night and collapsed into her car, her feet throbbing. There were cars lurking up and down each row, like vultures waiting to pounce on their prey. Determined not to be put off by this Katherine sat and munched on her sandwich and sipped her drink, she started to feel slightly human again. With relief she drove out of the centre thankful that she wasn't in the massive queue which now tailed all the way around the perimeter road of Bluewater and up and down the A2.

Her feet were still throbbing by the time she got home. She dropped the bags on the floor, popped the fish pie into the fridge, made a camomile tea to calm her and lay on a sofa with her feet propped up on one arm of the sofa. An hour later she felt revived and knew that she should go up to Wynenden Park to see Sir Geoffrey but she could not face it. The morning had been tortuous enough and whilst her mood had improved, she felt that a visit to him would be enough to put her in a foul mood again.

She felt restless, a need for fresh air and open spaces after the claustrophobia of the morning. Feeling guilty she changed into jeans and a warm jumper and put her walking boots on, on went the hat, the scarf, the gloves and the thick black waterproof coat. The cocooning of the walking boots soothed her feet and she wished she'd worn them shopping, going for comfort rather than style. Pocketing her keys and a torch as the evenings drew in so early, she hurried off up the road. Walking past the shops in the village she headed out in the direction of Wynenden School hoping that she would not be spotted by Sir Geoffrey or Lady Susan. Before reaching the entrance to Wynenden School she crossed the road and took a footpath across the fields.

She wondered what had happened during the interview DI Allix must have had with Robert Codell the previous evening. Had he found out whether Robert had been abusing Cecilia? Had he denied it? If he had abused Cecilia and he denied it would they ever be able to prove what he had done?' She was deep in thought when she reached the lane she needed to cross in order to join the next section of the footpath. The sun was starting to lower itself in preparation to set and she knew she needed to hurry if she were to be back in the village before dark. She climbed over the style and walked down the lane towards where she would find another style and be able to join up with the next footpath. She stood aside to let a car go past, not looking to see who was approaching. The car pulled up beside her and her heart sank.

Chapter Nineteen

'You need to be careful out here on your own, these lanes are awfully narrow, wouldn't want anything to happen to you if a driver didn't see you.'

Katherine shivered, was he threatening her again? It was Andrew Battle in his Range Rover. She slipped her hand into her pocket and subtly felt around for her mobile. With horror she realized she had not picked it up from the kitchen work surface.

'Afternoon Andrew,' she said politely, trying to hide her nerves. He grinned at her.

'Decided to sell yet? Another body. Tut, tut, people are going to think you are storing them up there,' he laughed at his own sick joke.

How could anyone be so unpleasant? Had he had no feelings for Cecilia, the girl he had had sex with on numerous occasions? Had he no respect for the dead? She looked at his self-satisfied face, his perfectly groomed physique dripping in wealth and something snapped inside her.

'Have you no respect for the dead? For that poor girl and her baby?' she snapped furiously. 'Your baby,' she snarled.

A startled look swept fleetingly across his face, his eyes flashed dangerously. 'What are you talking about? You're determined to get me into trouble with the police, you and your *false* accusations,' he emphasized.

'False! You confessed to me that you had slept with her on many occasions. Just because she's not here to defend herself you think you can get away with it! She was under aged, or did that not mean anything to you?'

He sneered at her. 'You can't prove anything. And just to make it perfectly clear to you, I did not kill her or her baby.'

'But you were seen,' Katherine blurted out the lie before she could stop herself, he'd infuriated her so much she couldn't help it.

His eyes narrowed and pierced into her. 'You're making it up. Besides, so what if I was seen with her?'

'You met her at the farmhouse on the day she went missing, didn't you?' she noticed that he had shifted uneasily in his plush cream leather seat. She had no idea where these ideas were coming from, but having started she had to pursue them. She was sure he was lying.

His face changed back to a smirk. 'You think you've got it all sussed don't you? You think I murdered her? Hah!' he laughed. 'Why would I murder her? She was nothing to me! Sure she was a good screw and a bit of fun but that was it, end of.'

'So why did you go to the farmhouse?' Katherine was convinced that her gut feeling was right, she knew he was hiding something, but murder? That she was not so sure.

He stared intently at her for a few moments, weighing up his options. 'Well, no one is going to believe you and you can't prove anything, I know you're lying about me being seen. She phoned me, said she needed to see me urgently. Of course, I thought she wanted to re-kindle our acquaintance, there seemed to be a certain irony to me that she wanted to meet at the farmhouse. I wanted that house, why not baptize it with my pleasure early?'

Katherine shuddered in disgust and tried to push the unsavoury images away which were popping into her head.

'When I got there I found that she had this squawking baby with her. I was furious. I'd cancelled a meeting to see her, she wasn't up for it, far from it. Said the baby was my son. I told her to get stuffed, I wanted nothing to do with her or the baby She said if I paid her twenty grand in cash by that afternoon she need never see me or the baby again, she'd disappear and I'd never hear from her again.'

She must have known what his reaction would be, thought Katherine, sure that he would want nothing to do with her or the baby.

'I laughed at her, told her she had to prove it was mine and then come after me for money. There was no way I was going to pay a penny to her, I was livid, left her to it and never saw her again.' His gaze had drifted off whilst he spoke.

Katherine was stunned that she had been right. That her wild guess of him seeing her at the farmhouse on the day she disappeared was correct. Her mind was racing with unanswered questions, then spoke. 'When was this? When did you see her? Morning? Afternoon? Evening?'

'Mid morning, why?'

'Because if you saw her and you didn't kill her, then whoever came after you must have. Did you tell the police this when she went missing?'

'You must be joking! Why would I do that? Besides, she told me she was going to disappear. I assumed she had done that, done what she said she was going to do.'

'Did you see anyone else? Anyone when you left?' she asked hopefully.

He frowned then shook his head. 'No. There was no one about. I passed Geoffrey in the lane, had a chuckle to myself, he would have been furious if he'd seen my car at the farmhouse.'

'And that was it, no one else?'

'No. Now I've wasted enough of my time. Tell the police what you like, they can't prove anything and I will deny it all anyway. Soon enough they'll believe that they have a deluded female on their hands.' With that he closed his window and roared off.

They wouldn't would they? Katherine was worried. If she told DI Allix what Andrew had just told her he might start thinking that she was wasting his time, that it was self-interest and she had some kind of personal vendetta against Andrew.

As she walked back across the fields in the growing dusk, Katherine's mind was crammed with questions. If Andrew had been summoned to meet her at the farmhouse, who else had? Who was the father of the baby? Was it Tom? Andrew? Robert? Had Robert Codell met her there? Had he been abusing her or was it untrue and a pack of lies? Who had the most to lose by the revelation that they had had sex with an under aged girl? Her answer to this one had to be Robert. He was her teacher, ten years ago he was about to be appointed Deputy Head and was no doubt ambitious and had his eyes on a Headship some-where. If it came out that he had had a relationship with

198

one of his pupil's, let alone an under aged one, he would be ruined, he would surely be jailed and his career as a teacher would be well and truly over. But what if it's not true? What if Cecilia made it up? Who would have the most to lose? Katherine's gut feeling was that Andrew was not guilty, he was too arrogant and Cecilia's threat to expose him would be seen as an irritation rather than anything else. Or would it?

So deep in thought was she, that she arrived back home without having been aware of getting there. The more she puzzled, the more questions popped up, she was sure she was missing something. Should she tell DI Allix of her conversation with Andrew? She decided to sleep on it and call him in the morning after her visit to see Sir Geoffrey.

Chapter Twenty

Katherine braced herself for her meeting with Sir Geoffrey, why she felt nervous she did not know. A thought had sprung into her head overnight. If Andrew had seen Sir Geoffrey driving up the lane in the opposite direction, maybe Sir Geoffrey had seen someone arriving at the farmhouse or driving down the lane towards it? She knew it was ten years ago but was hopeful that he might remember something, anything.

She pressed the bell and waited. Again it was some time before she heard the approaching barks of the dogs. They arrived in a clatter at the door before anyone else and she saw the dogs' heads popping up and down as they barked and jumped to see who it was. She was delighted when Ted appeared and opened the door.

'Hello. I thought you might be busy on the Estate?'

'I was, but Sir Geoffrey asked me to come in.'

'Oh, right. How are they?' she asked tentatively, trying to ascertain the mood that Sir Geoffrey and Lady Susan were in, for she felt sure that his wife would be there too.

Ted frowned and searched for the right word. 'Tense, I think, is how I would describe them.'

'Tense? But why?' This did not bode well for their meeting she felt.

'I...' he thought better of it, 'I'm not entirely sure.'

Katherine still wasn't really sure why she was here. She had no information that would be of use to them and felt that their time would be better spent in talking to the police. Ted led her through the myriad of corridors again until they arrived at the same drawing room they had been in on Katherine's last visit. He held the door open for her and she walked into the room which, fortunately, was warmer than the rest of the house, as it had a blazing log fire roaring in the fireplace. Sir Geoffrey was pacing up and down and Lady Susan was sitting down, gazing into space. Sir Geoffrey turned and greeted Katherine as she entered and ushered her to a seat.

'Be a good chap Ted and make us some coffee will you.' It was an order rather than a request.

With Ted dispatched to do as he was told, Sir Geoffrey stood astride in front of the fire warming his back and looked intently at Katherine. She shifted uncomfortably under his gaze. Lady Susan, Katherine observed, looked deflated, not her usual robust, jolly hockey sticks, type of self. After a moment Sir Geoffrey spoke.

'So, Katherine,' he said, 'more rum goings on at the farmhouse eh?'

'Yes. I'm afraid so.'

'Tell me, what happened?'

She looked from one to the other, both were focused entirely on her. 'Well, I, um, don't know really. I wasn't there. I received a phone call from my builder asking me to come to the farmhouse as quickly as possible and that the police were on their way. When I got there the police had already arrived,' she paused unsure as to what they wanted.

Sir Geoffrey cleared his throat. 'And did you,' his voice trembled slightly, 'did you see the baby?'

Katherine noticed that at the mention of the baby Lady Susan gripped her hands tightly and her face took on a frozen appearance. Katherine closed her eyes and shuddered at the memory. 'I didn't see the baby itself. I didn't want to. I just saw a blue bundle and then I left the room.'

'Just tell me about the bundle. What was it like?'

Katherine shivered at the question. Why was he so intent on getting information about the baby? It didn't seem right to her, but she dutifully answered the question as best she could. 'It was small and wrapped tightly, though I think an edge of the blanket had come loose when it was, um. You know. Er. Discovered.'

Fortunately, she was temporarily saved from further questions as Ted arrived with a tray laden with coffee and some digestive biscuits. Katherine gratefully took her cup and saucer, filled with instant coffee, and clung to it as though it were a security blanket.

'Is there any more you can tell us about the baby?' persisted Sir Geoffrey who had now sat down next to his wife.

Ted caught Katherine's eyes and raised his eyebrows questioningly and she gave an imperceptible shrug in response.

'Not really. I think the police are the ones you should talk to, they will have more information. Oh,' she suddenly remembered, 'other than the fact that it was a boy.'

'How can the police be so sure that the young girl was the baby's mother?'

'Well, they obviously have to wait for DNA tests to be carried out to confirm it, but lying close by to the baby was a necklace which had been given to Cecilia for her sixteenth birthday by her parents. Her mother has also confirmed that the blanket is identical to the one Cecilia had with her when she took the baby out.'

A silence fell and Sir Geoffrey and Lady Susan looked at each other, sharing something, but Katherine knew not what.

'It's very sad,' said Ted quietly. 'Poor girl. Poor baby.'

Katherine sighed. 'Terrible.'

'Actually,' Katherine decided to plunge straight in, 'I know that Cecilia and the baby were at the farmhouse on the day she went missing and I understand, Sir Geoffrey, that you drove up the lane that day? I don't suppose you saw anyone? Anything? Anything at all which might help the police? Cecilia had met someone at the farmhouse, he or she may not have anything to do with her murder but they might unknowingly hold a vital clue.'

'Did you call the police, Ted?' asked Sir Geoffrey suddenly sounding weary.

Katherine was startled. Police? If he'd called the police? Why had she had to come up here?

'Yes I did Sir Geoffrey. DI Allix will be here sometime later this morning.'

It was Katherine's turn to look questioningly at Ted. He, in turn, shrugged and mouthed that he didn't know why.

'Are you sure there's nothing else you can remember Katherine,? Nothing else about the baby?'

'No. Really I don't. I'm not sure what you want to know? Why are you so interested in the baby?' she asked, being slightly impertinent.

Sir Geoffrey gazed at his wife. She took his hands, squeezed them and nodded. 'Go on,' she whispered hoarsely, 'everyone will know sooner or later.'

What on earth is going on? Again she raised her eye-brows at Ted who gave her a "I really don't have a clue" look back

Sir Geoffrey got up and went to a beautiful antique, ma-hogany, bureau and took out a piece of paper. He handed it to Katherine, who studied the piece of paper and felt con-fused, as though she were being particularly dense. She handed it to Ted who studied it too. He then looked up at Sir Geoffrey, a look of comprehension in Ted's eyes.

'I'm sorry. I don't understand? What has this got to do with the ...' her voice trailed off. Oh my goodness! It couldn't? He couldn't? But how? She gaped at Sir Geof-frey astounded.

He sat down next to his wife and hung his head in shame. His wife gripped his hands in comfort.

'You're the, you're the ...' she stuttered. He nodded. Katherine looked at Ted who was shell shocked.

'Are you sure? I mean, I don't understand?' there was anger starting to build in her now. How could he? How could he do it?

'Yes.'

Katherine and Ted sat in stunned silence for a few min-utes trying to get their heads round what had been revealed to them.

'Why don't you explain. Start from the beginning,' prompted his wife gently.

He cleared his throat and ran his finger round the inside of his shirt collar nervously. 'I thought she was older. She looked it, looked nearer to twenty from what I could tell,' he glanced apprehensively at his wife who nodded, encouraging him to go on.

'I. We. We'd had a huge argument. Like one we'd never had before, nor since. I was furious, absolutely livid, I stormed out and marched across the estate. I ended up at the farmhouse, I had a bottle of Scotch with me, I'd swiped it in fury. Thought I'd go into the farmhouse and quietly get sozzled. Anyway, I go in only to find this girl in there, crying her eyes out she was, her face was red, nose raw, eyes swollen. I was in such a bad mood I shouted at her for trespassing, which made her cry even more. I can't cope with tears, too emotional for me, got to keep those things in. I offered her my bottle of Scotch and she took a swig then produced a bottle of vodka she had with her. She wouldn't tell me what precisely was wrong, just said her life was a mess, how she hated everything around her, hated her family, she seemed to hate life in general. I assumed she'd had a row with her boyfriend or whatever, usually the cause of being over emotional in a female. We got through the Scotch and started on her bottle of vodka. We got pretty drunk.' He cleared a frog from his throat and glanced nervously at his wife again, she gripped his hands and looked intently at him. 'The next thing I knew... I woke up a few hours later and I was,' he blushed heavily and ran his finger round the collar of his shirt again, 'I was not er, terribly well, er, attired, should I say.'

Katherine and Ted gaped in astonishment, their mouths hanging open.

'Anyway, made a complete fool of myself. Thoroughly ashamed of my behaviour. Told Susie straight away. Never had secrets from her and wasn't about to start. Susie was a jolly good girl about it, forgave me. I didn't deserve it, but she forgave me,' he said gruffly, showing publicly the most affection for his wife that he had ever done. 'Thought that was the end of it. Moved on. Until I had a phone call from the girl months later, said she had to see me, it was important and I had to meet her that day. 12 o'clock she said. As you can imagine, I had no desire to see her, let alone go to the farmhouse where my, shall we say, indiscretion, occurred. Spoke to Susie and we decided I should go, see what she wanted. Susie knew she could trust me. Never had been unfaithful before and wasn't going to be again. A silly drunken mistake. Haven't touched a drop of the hard stuff since.'

'So you were on your way to see her,' thought Katherine out loud.

'Yes. I met her. She seemed a lot younger than previously. With her was a tiny baby. In warm clothes, he was dressed all in blue. She'd put the changing mat on the dusty oak floor and the blue blanket on top of that and he was lying on that, looking around, little legs kicking,' he drifted off at the memory. 'She told me he was mine, that I was the father. She needed money. She was going to stay with friends but she needed money for the baby and needed it that afternoon. I don't think she expected me to be interested in the baby, but I was. It was something I, something *we*,' he corrected himself, 'had always wanted, a son and heir. There he was. I couldn't believe it! Out of such a mistake came something so precious. I told her I wanted to be involved in his life, that he would be the heir to the Es-

206

tate. But despite being bowled over and stunned by the events I still held on to reality. I knew that if she could have a drunken, er, whatever, with me, then it wasn't beyond the realms of possibility that she could do it with someone else. I had to have proof that he was mine. She told me that she needed some money and that when she got back we could sort it all out, maintenance and the like. I explained that it would take a day or two to get some cash for her, it's common knowledge that we're asset rich but cash poor. I couldn't rustle up a few thousand just like that. Besides, I needed to speak to Susie, she needed to be involved, to be alright about the situation. She said she needed the money again, was quite agitated about it, there was nothing I could do, I simply could not get my hands on such money so quickly. I told her she should give me a ring the next day and I would let her know when the cash would be ready. Eventually she accepted what I was saying and said she would call me. The baby was crying by now so I asked if I could pick him up. She hadn't named him. I asked if he could have one of my family names, it was a tradition. She didn't object but was vague. She let me pick the baby up. He was so tiny, so fragile, it was incredible to think that the small infant I held in my hands was mine. My flesh and blood,' his eyes sparkled at the memory. 'He had a sharp little nail so she carefully bit it off. I asked if I could have it, she thought it was weird but agreed. He wobbled as I held him, his neck so floppy, I stroked his hair, it was only afterwards that I realized one of them had clung to my jacket. I calmed him down a bit but she insisted she had to feed him and could I leave. So I did. Told her she could stay there as long as she liked. My mind was whirring with plans, if he was my baby I wanted to be involved, wanted Susie to be involved. I knew in my heart when he looked into my eyes that he was mine. I told her to phone me the next day. I knew she lived in the village, I'd asked her for her address, her phone number but she said she didn't want to give them to me, her parents weren't happy about her having had the baby. She said it would take them time to get used to the idea of her being a mother, but that when the time was right she would tell them who the father was. I accepted this, I was in shock. You don't expect to wake up one morning and have your world turned upside down do you?' He looked questioningly at them.

Feeling as though she was on the set of a movie and that this was all make believe, Katherine felt that her mind was about to explode from information overload. Ted sat there still looking stunned. He'd worked for his employees for ten years and never in a million years would he have expected this.

'What time did you leave her?' asked Katherine, as her brain processed what she had been told and segments started to fall into place.

'It was probably about 2 o'clock. She was alive and well and so was the baby. I came straight back here and told Susie. I showed her the sliver of finger nail and the hair and it was she who suggested they be sent off for DNA testing, it would cost, but it would be worth it to be one hundred percent sure that he was my son. Susie could see things more clearly, was more practical. She's been an absolute rock. Arranged for a couple of thousand pounds in cash to be ready for collection the next day, thought that was enough for nappies, clothes and the like, keep the baby going. She went and collected the cash the next morning whilst I waited for the girl to telephone me. We had discussed the situation. We wanted to be involved in the baby's life, wanted the baby to know his heritage. I waited and waited for her to call, the cash was ready, but she never called. Susie went down to the village to see if she could find her, thought it would be more subtle than me going. She heard a whisper in the post office that the girl had gone missing. There was no talk of the baby. We didn't know what to think, maybe the girl had gone early, thought she'd be in touch. The girl's mother called the police in, it was then that we discovered how old she was, that she was sixteen. I was stunned and horrified, I had no idea, she looked so much older. We were both still convinced that she had gone to her friends early, assumed that if her parents were having to adjust to their daughter being a mother and weren't happy about the situation, that she might have found life at home too hard. After a week the village got together and started searching the surrounding area, I got Ted to organize staff from the estate to search every inch of it. I checked the farmhouse. There was no sign of them and nothing seemed disturbed but it must have been. To think that they were bricked up there, how could I not have noticed? We waited and waited in the hope that she would contact us, that she would get in touch, time passed and we worried that something really had happened to her, but we never gave up hope. The hope that, one day, my son would walk through the door. Susie sent the nail clipping and hair off for analysis and eventually it came back confirming what we had suspected, that the baby was mine, I was the father.'

'Did you not tell the police about the baby?'

He shook his head. 'No. Like I said, we assumed that she had gone to stay with her friends, we didn't want to make things worse for her, and then, as time went by, it was harder to do so. Foolish, totally foolish, we should have told the police everything right from the start, maybe,' he choked, 'maybe my son would still be alive and the girl would be too.'

'I don't think so, I don't think you could have done anything. It's believed both she and the baby were murdered that day. Which is why, if there is anything, absolutely anything, no matter how insignificant a fact, you need to tell the police and you need to tell them what you have just told us.'

The once stiff backed, brusque, sometimes pompous, sometimes arrogant, but on the whole kind man, looked small and deflated. Katherine admired Lady Susan for standing by her man, for putting her faith in him, but was not overtly surprised as she was of the dying breed who stood by their man no matter what, who took their marriage vows and stuck to them – for better, for worse, for richer, for poorer – Katherine felt humbled. Perhaps there was more she could have done to save her marriage? But when the husband runs off with another woman and doesn't want to return and stick to the commitment he made to his marriage, there was not a lot that could have been done.

'I know. That's why I asked Ted to contact the police. I will do *anything* humanly possible to find out who killed my son and did the same to that poor girl. I will not rest until justice is done,' he sat up slightly and held his head high, determination surrounding him like an aura.

Katherine understood now why she had been summoned. The first time, when Cecilia had been found and Sir Geoffrey kept asking if there was anything else, he was obviously asking about his son. Perhaps the fact that the baby had not been found with his mother had maintained their hope that his son was still alive? Living the life of a happy ten year old? For the body of the baby to be found must have been devastating, though perhaps not entirely unexpected, the hope whipped away from them in a flash. If Sir Geoffrey was the father, had Tom known about it? Had he somehow found out? Having dismissed him in her own mind as a suspect, he now came to the forefront. What would he have done if he had found out that his girlfriend had slept around? That he was not the father of her child? Was she really going to go to France with him? Or was she going to go on her own? Katherine only had his word that the plan was they would both go. Had he told the police yet what he had told her?

'Katherine?' she became aware of Ted trying to get her attention.

'What? Oh, sorry, I was thinking, there's a lot to take in.' It was clear to her that Sir Geoffrey had had no idea Cecilia was fifteen when she became pregnant. Presumably the DNA test would be done again? She was sure he was telling the truth and that it wasn't the DNA test for another baby, but the police would need confirmation. Would Sir Geoffrey be arrested? Be charged with illegal activities? The situation was too dreadful, a complete mess and what would Cecilia's parents do when they found out? What would the whole village do? Would it ostracize them both? Would Susie suffer because of her husband's one indiscretion? If Tom didn't know, how would he take it?

Katherine had a nagging ache beginning in her head and she was sure it was going to turn into one of the worst headache's she'd ever had. Her blood was pumping athletically around her body, as though she had just run a marathon and she felt slightly light headed. She focused and found both Sir Geoffrey and Lady Susan peering at her with concern.

'Are you alright Katherine?' asked Lady Susan speaking for the first time. 'You look awfully pale. I've sent Ted off to make some more coffee, I'll put extra sugar in yours, you look like you need it, for the shock.'

Katherine smiled weakly and wondered in amazement at how Lady Susan could put the needs of Katherine before the agony that she must be going through. She must surely be aware of what was going to happen? The consequences? The pin had been pulled out of the grenade and all she could do was wait for it to explode.

It wasn't long before Ted returned, this time with large mugs of coffee, something for them to all grip on to. Lady Susan added several spoons of sugar to them all and whilst it tasted disgustingly sweet, Katherine found a strange comfort in it.

Sir Geoffrey had spent the last few minutes pacing up and down, his brow furrowed in deep thought. His wife patted the seat next to her and he obediently sat down and took the mug of coffee offered to him. 'It's no good,' he said, 'I can't think of anything that could be of use to the police. I really wish I could.'

'Is there nothing? Did you drive straight home? Saw nothing? Saw no one?'

He frowned again, working through his journey back from the farmhouse, it was ten years ago which didn't help.

'I got into the car, was in a bit of a daze, turned left and drove up the lane, saw that chappy, who is now Headmaster at the school, out for a walk, got home, spoke to Susie. That was it.'

Katherine had frozen when he'd mentioned "that chappy" could it be a coincidence that he was there? That he was near the farmhouse? 'Do you mean Robert Codell when you say "that chappy"?' she asked trying to keep the tremble from out of her voice.

'Yes. That's the one. Jolly good fellow. Ah,' Sir Geoffrey's eyes lit up, 'maybe he saw something?'

'Possible,' Katherine managed to croak. There was no doubt in her mind now that she had to tell DI Allix about Andrew Battle. If he were telling the truth that he had seen Cecilia first. Then Sir Geoffrey had seen her next. Could it have been Robert Codell? She felt a chill go down her spine and she gripped her mug tighter.

In the distance the dogs started to bark and a faint ring was heard. Ted went to answer the door and returned a few minutes later with DI Allix and DS Wilson. If DI Allix was surprised to see Katherine there he did not show it. She could see Sir Geoffrey and Lady Susan bracing themselves for what lay ahead. Katherine excused herself, smiling wanly at Sir Geoffrey and Lady Susan and murmured to DI Allix that she needed to speak to him. He promised to call and she left them to it. Ted guided her through the ancient building to the front door. They stood looking at one another, still in a state of shock over Sir Geoffrey's revelation.

'Will I see you tonight?' Ted asked hopefully.

Katherine frowned for a moment before remembering that they were supposed to be going for a drink that evening. 'Er. Yes. I've got this dreadful headache, so assuming I can get rid of it, yes.'

'How about I cook you supper instead? Save you having to do it yourself and my house will be quieter than a noisy pub?'

'That would be nice, thank you.' It would also give them the opportunity to talk about the days dramatic turn of events without fear of someone overhearing them and spreading it around. Discretion was of the utmost, Katherine felt.

'Would you like me to pick you up? You could have a drink then?' He looked quizzically at her.

'No, thanks, I'll be fine. What time would you like me to come over?'

'Sevenish? Whenever suits you, I'll be there.'

'OK, see you later then.'

On autopilot she drove home, took a couple of paracetamol and lay down on her bed, her head banging so loudly it felt like it was being used as a drum. She drifted in and out of sleep, vaguely aware of her head calming but waking when it started pounding ferociously again. She took two more paracetamol and drank a couple of glasses of water then went back to bed. By 5 p.m. she awoke again, her head pounding less, but unsettled by the dreams and semi-consciousness she had drifted in and out of, everything to do with Cecilia was being spun round like a washing machine on full spin. Robert Codell was the unknown quantity, until she knew for definite whether he had been abusing Cecilia or not she would not know whether he had the motive to kill her. She reminded herself that he could be innocent. That it could be made up. Information like that, if incorrect was dangerous and damaging, the potential to ruin one man's life and his family was easily done in one quiet, whispering rumour. The damage done, trust lost and suspicion prevalent. There would be no case of "innocent until proven guilty" in the position he held, people would automatically assume him guilty.

Groggily she got up and had a shower, letting the warm water run down her and wash away the griminess which she felt. She washed her hair vigorously, endeavouring to remove the nagging headache which still lurked at the back of her head. She slipped on a casual dress, nothing too dressed up, with long sleeves, a scoop neck and soft fabric which wrapped itself around from the front underneath the bust and tied in a bow at the back. The fabric was a mix of blues and greens in a small swirly pattern and flowed loosely around her. Her stomach rumbled as she had not had anything to eat since breakfast, by now it was 6 p.m, not wishing to spoil her appetite, but unsure of what time Ted would serve supper, she munched on a piece of toast and restrained herself from having several more pieces as it had whetted her appetite. She took another couple of paracetamol and hoped that they would be enough to finally dispose of her headache.

Ted's house was a small farmhouse on the edge of the Wynenden Park Estate, it came with the job. Katherine pulled up in front of the picturesque house, a slightly smaller version of the one she had bought, but in good condition. The door opened and a black Labrador came bounding out. 'Ella!' commanded a voice, ensuring that the dog came to an obedient halt rather than jump up at Katherine. The dog wagged her tail enthusiastically and Katherine stroked her head and murmured to her.

'Sorry. Meant to keep her in but she beat me to it!'
laughed Ted.

'Oh, she's lovely, very friendly.'

'You ok with dogs then?'

'Grew up with them, just never owned one myself because I was always working, didn't think it was fair to keep a dog cooped up all day.'

He grinned, relieved. Ella was a major part of his life and it was important that anyone who came into his life liked dogs too. 'Come in, it's freezing out here.' He ushered into the kitchen and took her coat.

Katherine was surprised at how neat and tidy the house, from what she could see, was. She'd expected a bachelor pad to be filled with junk; no surface clear, chaos reigning. So it was most pleasant to see the kitchen tidy, work surfaces with food or cooking implements on them rather than piles of unwashed dishes and neglected paperwork. The old oak units had a refined air about them despite having seen better days, they suited the age of the house. There was an ancient dark blue Aga emitting warmth on the far side of the room with pots simmering on the top.

'Drink?' he asked.

'Something soft please.'

'Apple juice, orange juice or elderflower cordial?'

'Elderflower please.' She sat at the rectangular oak kitchen table and watched him as he deftly poured the drinks, got the ice out then checked the food on the Aga.

'Smells delicious,' she commented.

'Thanks. Hope it's ok. Didn't know what you liked and forgot to ask you this morning. You're not vegetarian are you?' he looked panic stricken.

'No, don't worry, love veggie food but I love meat too.'

Relief spread over his face. 'Phew! I did try and phone you this afternoon but you must have been out.'

'Sorry, I collapsed on the bed, my head was so bad, had a bit of a snooze, didn't hear the phone ring and I completely forgot to check the answer phone.' She wondered if she'd missed a call from DI Allix.

'How's your head now?'

'Much better thanks. So what did you decide on in the end?' she nodded towards the Aga.

'Roast lamb, roast potatoes, veg, gravy, hope that's OK?'

'Mmm, delicious! And I am very impressed that you can cook.'

'Don't speak too soon, you haven't tried it yet!'

There was a momentary lapse in conversation which Katherine eventually broke. 'How did it go after I left this morning?' she asked tentatively.

His face saddened as he thought of his employers. 'Difficult. DI Allix was as surprised as we were, though he did a good job of keeping a neutral face. Sir Geoffrey told them exactly what he had told us. He accompanied them down to the station to make a statement, which took a while, I drove him and waited. Of course what was worse, and something I don't know if he will recover from, was when he was told that Cecilia was just fifteen when she conceived their baby. I genuinely don't think he had a clue that she was so young. He's a real gentleman, he would *never* knowingly have had sex with her if he had known she was under aged, alcohol or no alcohol, intoxicated or not. I still can't believe he did what he did in the first place, it's so out of character. So unlike him. Unfortunately no one's going to believe him, once this gets out I dread to think what's going to happen.'

Katherine shook her head sadly at the whole situation. The hard fact was that he would be classed as a paedophile, the point that he had no idea she was under aged, that it wasn't pre-mediated, not calculating, was consenting by both parties – albeit drunkenly - and a one off indiscretion in an unblemished record of fidelity, would be irrelevant. 'What are you going to do?'

He shrugged and looked lost. 'I don't know. I don't know how the rest of the staff will take it, what their reaction will be? On the plus side most of them have worked for him for twenty or thirty years, they should know him, know that it was completely out of character. However, security could be an issue. There's not enough money to pay for increased security, so if people come onto the Estate to cause trouble, to get to Sir Geoffrey,' he shuddered. 'I'm going to have to do the best I can and more.'

She didn't envy him one bit, it was going to be ugly there was no doubt about that. 'This all happened shortly after you started. Did you not think there was something strange in his behaviour?'

'I've asked myself that a million times, but I was new to the job, I didn't really know Sir Geoffrey and Lady Susan and they're not the type of people who wear their hearts on their sleeves. It takes a while to build up a relationship and trust of people like that. If I'd been with them for ten years at that time then yes, I think I would have picked up on something and I think they might have confided in me. They know they can trust me, that I won't betray them.'

'They're very lucky to have you, to have someone so loyal.'

'Thanks.' His face looked drawn and tired with worry. Katherine wanted to hug him, to make him feel better but she was apprehensive and nervous of the response she may receive, that he might reject her. 'Well, this supper is not going to cook itself. I'd better make the gravy.' He leapt up and into action.

'Anything I can do to help?' offered Katherine.

'Nope. You sit there and relax, there's not much left to do, I had it all ready. That's the beauty of having an Aga. I'll just make the gravy then serve.'

The food was delicious, the meat tender and succulent, potatoes crispy, Katherine felt herself being restored and the remnants of her headache drifted away as the stress from her body released itself. They spent the rest of the evening sitting at the kitchen table, long after the apple pie and custard had been finished. Well past midnight and with a wave of exhaustion hitting her she left, thanking Ted profusely and hesitated on the doorstep, unsure as to whether to kiss him or not. He kissed her softly on the cheek and she glowed all the way home.

Chapter Twenty-One

Tuesday morning was a glorious winter's day. A heavy frost covered the ground, the sky was pure blue and the sun strong. Katherine had discovered a message on her answer phone from DI Allix when she returned home the previous night. He said he would try to get hold of her on Tuesday and that it was all clear for the builders to go back to the farmhouse. She phoned Dougie as soon as she got up to let him know, rather apologetically, he informed her that his men were on another job for a few days which would be finished immediately before Christmas. He'd assumed that they would not be allowed back to the farmhouse until after Christmas and he needed to keep the money flowing in and the cash flow healthy. Disgruntled that Dougie had done this, she did reluctantly understand his reasoning but it meant further delays, every day mattered, at this rate her house wouldn't be finished before summer and she'd wanted to move in during the Easter holidays. He agreed to meet her for a quick chat at the farmhouse about mid morning, so she walked up there after breakfast, breathing in the clean, fresh, crisp air, clearing the cobwebs from her head.

He was there, ready and waiting for her, they briefly ran through a few points and discussed the kitchen. Katherine did her utmost to not think about the little bundle she had seen on her last visit, doing her best to force it from her mind, hopeful that when the works were complete it would eventually become a distant memory.

'I'll get the paint samples and drop them off here later along with brushes,' Dougie was saying. Whilst the house was in no way ready for samples to be painted onto the walls, Katherine felt the need to do something practical so that she didn't feel time was being wasted. Most of the house was going to be re-plastered and the samples would be covered up, but it would give her an idea of whether the colours she had selected would suit certain rooms or whether she needed a complete re-think. In some ways she felt that by painting the samples on the walls it would start to brush away the horrors of the previous months and bring a fresh start to the work.

'That'd be great, thanks. I'll come up tomorrow and make a start. If I don't speak to you before Christmas have a lovely one and I'll see you all back here next Wednesday.'

'Will do. You have a good one too Kitty. See you.' He hurried out leaving Katherine to absorb the silence which descended on the house. She leant on the ancient metal sink which, along with a wobbling strip of work surface, was all that was left of the old kitchen, and drank in the view of the overgrown garden and distant fields through the dusty window. The kitchen was south facing and the sun was just starting to edge its way round into the kitchen. Once the old kitchen was knocked through to the garden room light would flood in all day as it had windows on three sides facing east, south and west. The frost twinkled like diamonds in the soft winter sunlight, the acres of her land covered in a sparkling, crisp, white, blanket. She started to feel cold and zipped her coat up higher, then went out through the back door and locked up. The frost crunched under her feet as she walked around. Something made her glance up as she turned the corner of the building and was startled to see Robert Codell leaning on the gate at the entrance to the drive. He was gazing at the house and took a few moments before he noticed Katherine walking towards him, he turned to go, pretending he hadn't seen her.

'Hi!' called out Katherine loudly, determined not to miss her opportunity and contemplated what she might say.

He paused then turned back. He looked pale and tired, dark swathes were under his eyes and he seemed to have aged about ten years since she had last seen him. 'Hello,' he replied politely.

'Nice day isn't it?' continued Katherine.

'Mmm, yes,' was his vague reply.

'Would you like to have a look round?' asked Katherine suddenly feeling that if he found himself where the crime took place, it might jolt a memory, his subconscious making him blurt something out or at least prick his conscience if there was anything there which needed doing so. The amateur, and rather foolish, detective side of her coming out.

He looked confused. 'No. No thank you,' he turned to go.

'Are you sure? I thought you might like to see what's being done, particularly as you saw it before hand?'

His face froze and the muscles round his jaw tightened. 'No. Never been in it before,' he muttered.

Katherine pretended to look surprised. 'Really? I'm sure someone mentioned that you'd been in the house? Not for years though…' she looked vaguely off into the distance, pretending to recall some piece of information. 'I'm sure they said it was around the time that Cecilia went missing, but perhaps that was during the search for her?' She knew she was playing a dangerous game, but her god-children were her world and if the man standing in front of her had a fondness for young girls she was going to do everything to ensure that he did not remain in a position of responsibility with unlimited access to children. If she were wrong then she'd have to plead temporary insanity, stress, whatever he wanted to call it, and apologize – a lot - and hope that she, in turn, didn't get into trouble.

'Cecilia? I think you must be mistaken,' his voice had taken on a hard edge.

'Maybe I am, sorry, but I was sure someone said that you were up here on the day she disappeared? Must be my mind playing tricks on me, so much has been happening,' she tried to look innocent, weary and care worn and at the same time play the sympathy card.

He snapped. 'Look, I don't know what game you are playing but drop it. Understand?' He took a step closer to her and Katherine nervously felt for her mobile phone in her pocket and grasped her hand round it.

She took a deep breath and carried on, feeling a bit like someone poking a snake with a stick, waiting for the snake to strike. 'But you were,' she paused, 'close to Cecilia, weren't you?' her voice had dropped. She saw the fury in his eyes and tried not to flinch.

'I have no idea what you are talking about,' he replied through gritted teeth.

'You gave her extra English lessons didn't you?' it was a rhetorical question, 'except that you gave her a little more than extra English ...' her voice trailed off, the implication clear.

He leapt forward and grabbed her by the throat. 'You're playing with fire,' he hissed at her, his face so close that she could feel his garlicky breath on her face. 'She did nothing she didn't want to...' his voice trailed off and he shoved her back, glared at her and marched off down the lane, leaving Katherine shell shocked.

She stood stock still, her mind grinding slowly as she laboured to processes his words. Had that really just happened? He'd confessed, surely he had confessed? But it wasn't enough to convict him. He could deny it, say that he was referring purely to the English work. But she knew. She knew he was referring to far more than that. Her legs turned to jelly and she started shaking. She grabbed hold of the gate and lent heavily against it. Her head swam, breaths coming fast and furious, her heart pounding, she tried to take long deep breaths to calm herself but it made it worse. She lent her head against the gate waiting for it to pass, it took some minutes of focused, calm, breathing before her heart slowed a little and she stopped hyperventilating. She straightened up, closed her eyes and breathed deeply in through her nose and out through her mouth, she did this a few times until her heart started to slow further. With some clarity she used her mobile to put another call though to the police station, asking for DI Allix to phone as soon as possible.

She shut the gate behind her and hurried down the lane in the direction of the village, praying the Robert wasn't lurking down there waiting to do something to her. She glanced nervously about her as she went, walking as fast as she could so that she was almost running. She reached the Wynenden Road with relief and slowed to catch her breath. Katherine crossed over the road to the pavement and walked at a slightly slower pace through the village, feeling some modicum of security from having buildings around her. She had a sudden craving and need for a sugar fix and diverted into the post office. Fortunately Betty was not there and the other woman with whom she job shared was the total opposite to her work colleague, quiet, unassuming and uninterested in gossip. Katherine picked up a copy of The Times, a copy of the Christmas issue of the Radio Times and several bars of chocolate. She smiled and murmured pleasantries, paid quickly and as soon as she was out of the shop ripped the cover off a chocolate, caramel and biscuit bar and sank her teeth into the sweet chocolatey, biscuity, gooey confection. The sugar rush hit her and she felt her spirits rising.

She was about to turn into Wynenden Close when a car pulled up beside her. The passenger window went down and she saw Audrey Stillingfleet's pale face looking out at her. Despite the trauma she was going through she had still applied her full make up, though Katherine thought it wasn't quite as perfectly applied as it had been when she had seen her previously. 'Hello,' she said.

'Hello Audrey. How are you?' Katherine bent down to talk to her.

'Oh, you know. OK.'

'How's Rupert?'

Audrey's face darkened. 'Drinking even more. He's not been going in to work at all, which is perhaps a blessing given the state he is in, it's getting out of control and I don't know what to do about it,' her voice trembled.

Poor woman, thought Katherine, she had enough trauma to deal with over her daughter and grandson and was quite sure she could do without having to deal with a drunken husband, having to be strong for them both, run the business, the house, all the weight was on her shoulders and if she didn't get support soon, Katherine felt sure that Audrey would, unsurprisingly, have a breakdown. 'If you need to talk, you know where I am, call any time. Have you spoken to Rupert's doctor or your own doctor?'

'I tried. I even managed to persuade one of them to come out, didn't tell Rupert, but as soon as the doctor arrived Rupert stormed out. The doctor could see what state Rupert was in but there's not a lot they can do without his cooperation. I'm worried about his drink driving, what if he crashes into another car or someone else and kills them?'

'Have you mentioned this to DI Allix?'

'Yes, but unless they catch him drink driving there's nothing they can do. They don't have the resources to sit outside the house all day waiting from him to leave or return. They've far more important work to do.'

'I'm sorry I can't do more to help. You take care of yourself and please do call if you need anything.'

'Thanks Katherine. Bye,' with that she put her BMW into gear and drove off to clear up yet another mess of Rupert's making at work.

Poor, poor woman, thought Katherine gazing after her. What a miserable life she has got, no chance of any kind of a Happy Christmas for her, what has she got to celebrate? Nothing.   Katherine continued up Wynenden Close to home.

In desperate need of a caffeine fix when she got back, Katherine selected an extra strong coffee pod and popped it into her machine and watched it whir into life and fill her cup with the dark liquid. She gained comfort, as she usually found, from clutching the warm cup and sipping the hot liquid. She checked her answer phone and her mobile to make sure she had not missed a call from DI Allix and impatiently waited for him to call, couldn't he tell it was urgent? Having continued to pace up and down for an hour waiting for his call and restraining herself from phoning again, she decided to change her focus reasoning that "a watched pot never boils" and made herself cheese on toast. Flicking through the Radio Times she saw that the classic old film 'White Christmas' was on in half an hour, nothing like a bit of festive schmaltz to get into the Christmas spirit she thought. It was five days until Christmas Eve and definitely time to get on with wrapping presents, she brought them all down from the spare room, which was crammed with unpacked boxes like the rest of the house, and sat on the floor in the sitting room with White Christmas playing on the television. She focused herself totally on the task in hand to ensure that she didn't think about Robert or why DI Allix hadn't called. When a pile of enticingly wrapped presents sat neatly in the middle of the floor she made a cup of tea, took a shop bought mince pie from the cupboard and curled up on the sofa to watch the remainder of the film.

As the credits rolled there was a sharp rap on the door. Cautiously Katherine peered out of the sitting room window to see who it was, fearful that it might be Robert Codell even though he didn't know where she was currently living, it was DI Allix.

He smiled when she opened the door. 'Sorry it's taken a while for me to catch up with you,' he said pleasantly, 'but I've been a little bit busy as you could imagine.' He took up her offer of a cup of tea then settled himself on a sofa, laying his coat next to him. As dusk was falling, Katherine switched the lights on and drew the curtains.

DI Allix sipped his tea and waited for her to sit down. 'So, what was it you needed to speak to me about?'

Where did she start? So much had happened in the past forty-eight hours. She felt rather embarrassed about her behaviour now she was recounting her conversation with Andrew Battle and then moved on to Sir Geoffrey. DI Allix listened intently, nodding now and then and occasionally intercepting with a question.

She then paused, took a sip of her tea and broached the subject of Robert Codell. 'I don't know how far you've got with your enquiries? I saw you taking him away on Sunday evening.' She looked questioningly at him.

'I can't really discuss him with you, but suffice to say, as the main witness is dead it could be rather tricky to prove anything. We are however continuing to make enquiries.'

Katherine fiddled with her fingers, feeling rather foolish. 'I, um, I saw him this morning,' she said nervously, fearful that she would get into trouble for stirring things up. 'I was up at the house, had had a meeting with Dougie , I stayed at the house on my own for a little while then left. As I was leaving, I saw Robert leaning on the gate at the head of the drive, I know he saw me but he turned to go, so I called out to him. I... Well ... I didn't out rightly accuse him of, you know, with Cecilia, but I heavily hinted, talked about her extra English lessons, implied that he had given her more than the lessons...' her voice trailed off again. She looked anxiously at DI Allix who said nothing, feeling she was a complete idiot for doing what she'd done and trying to keep the embarrassed blush, which was creeping over her face, in check. 'Anyway, he denied ever having been up at the farmhouse and then he grabbed me around the throat and told me, and I use his precise words "She did nothing she didn't want to..." then he pushed me back and strode off. I know it was a really stupid thing to do, but I couldn't help myself, I don't know what came over me? I suppose the over protective side of me came out and my godchildren go to the Prep School and will probably go on the Senior School. I don't want them being at risk. I had to find out and by his reaction, his anger and what he said, I'm sure he abused Cecilia and maybe others.'

DI Allix sat silently for a minute, Katherine felt like a naughty child about to be reprimanded. 'I know you meant well,' he said with unnerving calmness, 'but it is best if you keep out of it. There's a difference between coming across information, which might be useful in an investigation, and deliberately goading someone into saying something they don't mean to. Whilst it would appear that the implication from the way he reacted, and what he said, would suggest an inappropriate relationship with Cecilia, there is no concrete evidence.'

'I know. I'm sorry. And I'm not a gossip. I won't go round saying things about people which aren't true and I'm only telling you this because you are the police and my priority is for the safety of my godchildren. Apart from anything, Robert Codell was seen not far from the farmhouse on the day that Cecilia disappeared. She could have contacted him, just as she did Andrew Battle and Sir Geoffrey, and demanded that he meet her at the farmhouse. Maybe she even asked him for money just as she had asked the others? After all, if he had abused her she wouldn't have to say much to remind him what a vulnerable position he was in, how one word from her could potentially mean the end of his career, mud sticks. I would say that that was a pretty strong motive for murder.'

'I understand. I really do and several lines of enquiry are being followed up. I must again ask you not to say anything about your thoughts on Robert Codell, or anything else to do with the case, to anyone, no matter how tempted, especially not to the parents of your godchildren. I don't have to tell you what the consequences would be if rumours abounded, true or not, his life would be ruined, an innocent man treated as guilty for something he may never have done. I don't want a witch hunt going on.'

'Don't worry, I won't, I will be keeping my eyes and ears open, but my mouth firmly shut,' she swiftly changed the subject. 'Do Audrey and Rupert know that Sir Geoffrey is the father of their daughter's baby?'

'Not yet. I want absolute proof before I break it to them. DNA tests are being carried out and as soon as I have the results I will tell them, I see no reason to not believe Sir Geoffrey but I have to be sure.'

'How are they? Sir Geoffrey and Lady Susan? You know that he thought Cecilia was older, twenty or so, he had no idea that she was under the legal age of consent. It *definitely doesn't* make it right, but I do feel for him and

Lady Susan. One moment of total out of character madness and stupidity could absolutely shatter their lives, more than it has already done, but then similar could be said for Cecilia. If she hadn't got pregnant she may still be alive.'

He restrained himself from giving her another lecture on interfering, hoping that she had listened and learnt her lesson. Annoyingly her interference had produced some interesting pieces of information, ones which the police had so far failed to tease out.

'It's a delicate situation and will be handled sensitively. I can't say any more than that I'm afraid.' He rose to go. 'Thank you for your help.'

Katherine saw him out and felt disquieted, she knew she was right and she was sure Robert was capable of murder.

Chapter Twenty-Two

Settling on a change of scene for the next morning, Katherine took herself off to the small town of Cranbrook some ten miles from Wynenden. It was a pretty little town with a strong community spirit centred around two roads which formed an "L" shape through the centre of the town. Along these were a wide ranging assortment of shops and banks, you could purchase pretty much anything you wanted to from haberdashery to food to clothes to jewellery and everything in between. Katherine wandered in and out of the shops picking up a couple of interesting kitchen implements in the well stocked cook shop, treating herself to a soft cream silk floaty top in one of the boutiques and then went for a cappuccino in the small Italian coffee shop and deli, the welcome was warm and the coffee excellent. It was packed and Katherine had to share a table with an elderly gentleman who was reading a newspaper. By the jovial banter which was batting backward and forward between him and one of the staff she assumed he was a regular.

She sat in the bay window which afforded her a view both up and down the bustling street and watched the world go by. There seemed to be a large number of over excited children, which was hardly surprising given that Christmas was only a few days away, their mothers looking slightly haggard and worn down by the whole event before it had even happened. It was nice to see a small town thriving, though there had been times of struggle and would no doubt be again, and keeping its individuality rather than giving in to the multitude of big brand shops which seemed to dominate so many high streets. On top of that was the bonus of free parking, a virtually nonexistent occurrence in this day and age. Katherine vaguely remembered reading something about the local council trying to introduce parking charges and there being a huge outcry against it, petitions were signed, letters written and with much celebration the proposal was over turned.

She suddenly spotted Robert and his wife Jane strolling down the street in deep conversation. Katherine turned inwards and prayed that they wouldn't see her let alone come into the coffee shop for a drink or something to eat. She waited a few moments before peeping round and breathed a sigh of relief as she saw their backs disappearing down the street. The last thing she wanted was a public confrontation and she had promised that she would steer clear of any antagonistic behaviour. Katherine gulped down the last of her cappuccino, paid and hurried up the street in the opposite direction to the one which Robert and Jane had just gone. She nipped into the paper shop and treated herself to a couple of glossy magazines and dose of Hello! magazine, plenty of fluffy reading to keep her going throughout Christmas. She had been so engrossed in the building works and brochures for the umpteen items which were required for the farmhouse, that she had had little time to flick mindlessly through such magazines. She always liked to have what she thought was a proper read before she went to sleep, a book to stretch her mind rather than something trashy to whizz through. The classics were her favourites, she loved a spot of Dickens or Hardy and even a splash of Dostoevsky from time to time. At the moment she was deep in her annual festive read of Dickens' much loved "A Christmas Carol" she could never resist reading it at this time of year and was now a firmly entrenched tradition for her.

With a pleasant and relaxing morning under her belt, she wolfed down the take away homemade soup and sandwich she had purchased in one of the delicatessens in Cranbrook, changed into a pair of old jeans, shirt, jumper and coat and set off to the farmhouse in her car, trusting that Dougie had delivered the paint samples and brushes to the farmhouse earlier as promised. She would have preferred a walk in what was yet another crisp, dry, day but if she were to get the samples up before dusk fell she wouldn't have time.

She frowned as she pulled up to the entrance to the drive. The gate was open and there was a black Porsche 911 sitting, parked haphazardly, abandoned in the drive. She was sure it wasn't Andrew's but couldn't place it. Katherine scanned the area and could see no one. She hesitated, perhaps she should go home or maybe she could phone Ted? What would she say to him though? That there was a strange car in the drive and could he come and help her? What a wimp, he would think she was, particularly when no doubt there would turn out to be a logical explanation. Even so, something unsettled her.

She locked her car door and kept the keys in her hand in her pocket, ready to use as a weapon. Her heart started to pound as she stepped silently, closer and closer to the house. She could hear nothing. She paused. Silence. She continued to creep, round the side of the house, silently approaching the back door, it was open and the kitchen window had been smashed. She froze on the spot. Dougie wouldn't have done that. Her breath was coming fast and furious. Very quietly she edged her way to the kitchen door and listened. Faintly she could hear a noise, it sounded like sobbing. Katherine strained to hear, there were moans mixed in amidst the sobs. She slid quietly through the gap in the kitchen door, breathing in so as not to nudge it and make it squeak. She edged slowly, stealthily, through the kitchen, walking round the rubble, the sound seemed to be coming from the winter sitting room. Quietly she crept, moving closer and closer until she was in a position to glimpse a figure through the open door.

There was a great lumpy mass sitting on the floor with his back to her, the collar of his black raincoat was pulled up high around his fleshy neck, his grey hair straggling over it. Surrounding him on the floor were empty bottles. She saw him tilt his head back and glug more from a still full bottle of whisky. She knew it was Rupert Stillingfleet and relaxed slightly. He was rocking backwards and forwards, sobbing and muttering words under his sob filled voice. Katherine hesitated, should she leave him to his grief? Or should she call Audrey to come and pick him up?

It felt intensely personal, too intrusive standing there listening to the poor man mourning the loss of his daughter and grandson. She decided to leave him for a while, but as she turned to creep out she accidentally tripped over a raised floorboard and fell against the wall. Rupert's hulk spun round. 'Sorry,' murmured Katherine.

'It's you,' he slurred, 'fancy a drink?' He waved the now half empty bottle at her. 'I've got plenty,' he flapped his hands towards a couple more full bottles of whisky. 'Come here, come and join me.'

Politely Katherine went over to him. He was sitting opposite the opened up fireplace. He pushed a bottle over towards her which she took and held on to, he was too drunk to notice whether she was consuming any or not. She sat in silence as he continued to mutter to himself, wondering what she should do? Maybe he needed someone to off load to?

'I'm sorry about Cecilia and about your grandson. I can't imagine how awful it is for you,' she said gently opening up the lines of communication, if talk was what he in fact wanted.

He swayed slightly as he sat there, his bloodshot eyes exacerbated by his tears and not focusing properly from the alcohol.

'So am I,' he slurred, 'she was my baby.'

Katherine nodded.

'Problem was, she was growing up, growing up you know. She wasn't my baby anymore.'

'I'm sure a lot of fathers feel like that about their daughters,' she encouraged.

'But she was mine! Mine, I tell you!' he shouted.

Katherine shifted nervously, hoping that the alcohol wasn't going to make him violent.

'She was my baby! How could I let anyone else have her? She was mine! How could she let anyone else touch

236

her? It wasn't right! She was for me, me alone!' he sobbed.

Katherine shivered. He couldn't? He surely couldn't be saying what she thought he was saying? Her heart slammed rapidly against her ribs and she felt bile rise up into her throat.

'Don't you see?' He swigged from his bottle and raw eyes looked pleadingly at her. 'She was mine to keep.'

Katherine tried to keep calm, but inside her head she was screaming "how could you do that to your own daughter?" it disgusted her to her core. She wanted to vomit. The thought of him touching her in that way. It was sick.

'Did I fail her? Could I not satisfy her? Is that why she turned to others?' he spat vehemently. 'I knew! I knew she slept with other men. That stupid boyfriend of hers to start with. There were others, I followed her. Secret liaisons all over the place. Why couldn't she be satisfied with me? I was the one who loved her, it should have *only* been me who touched her.' He took another long glug of whisky and threw the empty bottle skittling across the oak and picked up another, fumbling to twist off the lid.

A stream of swear words ran through Katherine's mind, along with panic, not knowing what to do.

'How could she get pregnant? It wasn't right! She needed to stay pure for me. Why did she have to dirty herself with other men? I could have provided her with everything! That baby,' he spat, 'she should have got rid of it, I arranged it all, make her pure again, for me, give her another chance, a chance to redeem herself but she had to come back with it, that devil child! She shouldn't have kept it. She had her chance and she blew it, she couldn't carry on, she ruined everything!' He took another swig.

Oh shit! Thought Katherine. He can't mean? She shoved her hand in her mouth and bit hard on it to prevent her from screaming.

'I followed her,' his eyes gazed at the fireplace, misty with the memories, 'saw her meeting that scum she called her boyfriend. Knew she'd be up here again, came up in the afternoon, all I could hear was the screech, screech, screech of that devil child, wouldn't shut up, I had to shut it up, I couldn't think, it was getting in the way, without it we had a chance, she could be my little girl again, she tried to fight me off, but it didn't take much to shut the baby up. Then she started screaming at me, shouting at me, I tried to make her feel better, held her to me, she struggled, but she knew better, she knew I could make her pure again, she felt me, we were one, but all she did was scream, she hit me!' he looked indignant.

Blood was dripping from Katherine's hand as she drew blood from biting so hard, tears streaming down her face, not from the pain, but from the evilness of what had been done.

He drank, long and hard from the bottle, it dribbled down his chin, but even when he finished he didn't seem to notice. 'I tried to get her to shut up, I did, I managed too but then she went limp in my arms, my baby, she shouldn't have struggled...'his voice trailed off.

Katherine sat rooted to the spot. If she ran, would he do the same to her?

'It's too late now. It's all ruined. She was supposed to remain here, resting in peace but you, you and your stupid builders ruined it! Everyone knows now that she's gone, they know about the baby, her purity gone. It's over.' He took another long swig and staggered to his feet. Katherine inwardly flinched not daring to move. He staggered out of the room and she heard him stumbling through the kitchen. She grabbed her phone and dialled the police station.

'Please, get DI Allix, anyone, up to Wynenden Farmhouse. NOW! Rupert Stillingfleet murdered his daughter Cecilia and her baby, he's here, hurry!' She broke off as Rupert staggered back into the room, Katherine cowered against the wall, but he swayed on the spot, leant over, swiped several times at a full bottle of whisky on the floor, finally grasped it and staggered out. She heard him again stumbling through the kitchen, then it went quiet. The blood was roaring in her ears and she was sweating profusely but shivering from cold. She caught a movement out of the corner of her eye through the window. He was stumbling towards his car. She couldn't let him drive in that state! Instinctively she ran out through the back door, round the house and up the drive as fast as she could.

'RUPERT!' she shouted. He turned and saluted her as he fell into his car. 'STOP!' He revved the engine of his Porsche, cranked it with a grinding into gear and put his foot down, then clumsily negotiated his way out of the drive, narrowly missing her car and the gates, swerving all over the road, she could hear the roar as he raced at terrifying speed up the lane. Katherine slumped on the ground and wept, not caring that the damp and cold from the grass was seeping through her jeans. Minutes later there was a squealing of brakes as several police cars flew into the drive.

DI Allix was amongst them. 'Where is he? Where's Rupert?' he asked urgently.

'You know?'

'He left a suicide note for his wife. Confessing to everything. She got it about half an hour ago, we were there when your call came through. Where did he go?'

'He went that way,' she pointed to the left, 'I tried to stop him, he's drunk so much, but I couldn't.'

'Stay here,' he commanded, indicating for a couple of police officers to look after Katherine. The rest of them jumped into their cars and drove off.

It was half an hour later before DI Allix returned, his face, worn, sad and defeated.

In the meantime a blanket had been wrapped round Katherine and she was sitting in the warmth of a police car. 'Did you find him?' she asked, fearing the worst.

He looked grim. 'Yes. He'd crashed his car into a tree, he's dead.'

Somehow Katherine had known, the way he had spoken, the way he had raced off, she could kick herself for not having tried harder, for not taking his keys off him earlier.

'There's nothing you could have done,' said DI Allix softly as though reading her mind. 'He'd planned this. If you had stopped him he would have found some other way to kill himself, maybe not now, but later.'

'Did his letter tell you everything?' her pained eyes looked deep into his.

'It did.'

She started at a sudden thought. 'What about Audrey? Did she know that he was abusing their daughter?'

'I would say from her reaction, no. She's not in a good way as you can imagine.'

'She's lost everything. Her daughter, her grandson and now her husband and all she has is the knowledge of what he did to her. Is anyone with her?'

'Her doctor is at the moment, she's had to be sedated.'

'So she doesn't know Rupert is dead yet? Poor, poor woman, how will she ever recover from this? Her life shattered, blown apart beyond recognition. This is the sort of thing you would expect to see in the vilest of movie's, the sort of film some sicko would go and watch,' she shook her head, her body and mind so numb with shock she could barely move.

'Let's get you home, into the warm,' he instructed the two police officers to take Katherine home and to stay with her. He in the meantime had to return to the crash site. The only ounce of relief in the situation was that Rupert had not killed someone else by his drunken driving, he had driven straight into a tree, deliberately DI Allix was privately convinced, the alcohol drunk in preparation to numb the last few breaths of life.

Chapter Twenty-Three

It was several hours later when DI Allix arrived at Katherine's house. She had persuaded the policeman and woman that she really was alright to be left on her own after she had changed out of her damp clothes and been plied with sweet tea. She sat shell shocked on the sofa, the darkness drew in and the sitting room was only lit by the occasional flash of car headlights coming up the road. With no lights on in the house, but her car on the drive - having been driven back by one of his colleagues - it was with trepidation that DI Allix knocked on her door. In a daze she dragged herself off the sofa and opened the door. She looked drawn and haunted. Guiding her back into the sitting room, DI Allix switched on a couple of lamps, drew the curtain and went into the kitchen to make some tea. Whilst the kettle was boiling he came back into the sitting room, picked up a rug which was over the arm of the chair and offered it to her, she was shivering even though the heating was on and she was well wrapped up in a thick jumper.

He handed her a mug of sweet tea and sat down opposite her. 'Do you feel up to talking?' he asked gently, 'it can wait until tomorrow.'

242

She shook her head. 'No. It's ok. I'd rather go through it now. Perhaps it will be cathartic?' She recounted from start to finish what had happened that afternoon, from the moment she drove up to the farmhouse to the arrival of the police.

'Thank you. Perhaps tomorrow, if you are feeling up to it, you could come down to the station and make a formal statement.'

She nodded. 'What did the letter say? The one Rupert wrote.'

It correlates with what you have told me. He mentioned the abuse, the murders, it was a rambling letter but it confirms - without doubt - that he was responsible.'

'It's so tragic, it's dreadful how one man's sick, twisted actions have such devastating consequences. He's ruined so many lives. How can anybody abuse their own child? It's pure evilness. Did Audrey really have no idea at all?'

'I don't think so. When she's fit enough to be interviewed we will have to question her, but I really don't think she was aware at all otherwise she would have tried to stop him. It's clear her priority has always been her daughter and I suspect she would have chosen her daughter over her husband.'

'But Cecilia's behaviour changed, surely she must have suspected something?'

'She put it all down to puberty, to hormones kicking in, the abuse didn't start until she was eleven.'

'Audrey's going to have to live with that for the rest of her life, always wondering "if only". How do you get over something like this?' Katherine shook her head in bewilderment.

'I don't know, it won't be easy for her, but hopefully with help and support, in time, things will become a little easier for her.' Sadly DI Allix knew that Rupert wasn't the only parent to abuse his child.

'So what happens now? What happens to Rupert?'

'As there is a signed confession and he confessed to you, albeit in a drunken state, the case will eventually be closed. Funeral arrangements for Rupert can go ahead as normal.'

'Who on earth is going to arrange it? Even if Audrey felt up to it, would she want to? He's taken away everything from her. I don't think many, if any, will attend his funeral, not after what he did.' She winced at the thought of what sort of gossip would be spreading around the village once it became public knowledge. She hoped that Audrey would not be ostracised for what her husband did, but Katherine knew that there would always be a few who would consider her guilty by association and responsible and not accept that she was as much a victim now as her daughter was then.

'Is there anyone I can call? Ask them to come and sit with you?' enquired DI Allix.

'No, I'll be fine. I'll give a friend a call once you have gone. Does Sir Geoffrey know yet? He ought to be told, you know, as he was the baby's father, though I assume you are still waiting for the DNA tests results you have requested?'

'Not yet, he's my next stop.'

'It might be an idea if Ted were present, as moral support, Sir Geoffrey has asked him to be present on other occasions. Would you like me to phone him for you?'

'That would probably be helpful, thanks.'

'And what about Tom? Does he know yet that it was Rupert who murdered his girlfriend? That Rupert was abusing her?'

'Not yet. After I've seen Sir Geoffrey I will go and see him.'

'Poor man. He said she was his true love, it's going to shatter him when he finds out that he wasn't the only man having sex with her, no doubt he'll feel betrayed and it will probably disgust him,' she shivered in revulsion at the thought of Rupert doing what he'd done to Cecilia.

'It won't be pleasant and even worse for him when, assuming we receive confirmation, he is told that the baby wasn't actually his. I'm not planning on breaking this to him until the DNA report has confirmed what Sir Geoffrey's report states.'

A thought struck her. 'So why was Andrew Battle so interested in the house? I had thought initially that it was because he had something to do with Cecilia's death, but in my last conversation with him he mentioned that he was already interested in purchasing the farmhouse at the time of her disappearance?'

DI Allix gave a small smile. 'I think I may have discovered the reason. He owns fifty acres of land which surrounds your property, the land is not held directly in his name but in one of many of his companies, though it is not easy to find this out. It appears he bought the land, which was not a recent part of the Wynenden Estate, with a view to developing it and creating a massive housing estate, houses all packed together, as many as he could fit in. The only problem was that, despite there being separate access to the site, the council deemed it as unsuitable for such a large development and in secret initial talks it was suggested that his best bet for getting the housing estate passed by the planners - allegedly along with a little palm greasing - was to purchase Wynenden Farmhouse and create an access through the land belonging to it. I imagine that the reason why Sir Geoffrey refused to sell to him was because he suspected Andrew might try and do something like that.'

'Ahh, no wonder he's so keen to get his hands on the farmhouse!' She smiled, then it faltered. 'Does that mean he is going to harass me until I sell the house and the land to him? Or even worse, what if he gets planning permission to build on the land he owns anyway?' She could see her country idyll, which was already teetering on the edge, being swallowed up by some monster estate.

'If he does continue to harass you, just let me know, he won't be allowed to get away with it. As for him getting planning permission to build on the land with the current access, it would be unlikely, even if he tried to slip it through the planning department it would become public knowledge and I doubt that anyone in the village is going to want a massive housing estate swallowing it up. Also, I think it is in a conservation area which should make it virtually impossible. He has gone to great lengths to hide the fact that he owns the land. I wonder how the village would feel if they discovered who the land owner really was and the true intention of its usage is?' His eyes twinkled at her.

She was slightly startled by his suggestion, but grinned at the thought. It truly would scupper Andrew's plans if the village found out, she didn't like to gossip, but if it were fact, nothing made up, a small comment casually dropped into a conversation for the greater good, would be round the village within minutes. It was certainly something for her to ponder upon.

'I'll see you at the station tomorrow then,' he got up.

'OK. Sometime in the morning. Whatever time suits you just let me know, I'd rather get it over and done with then try and forget about it as much as I can. I'll give Ted a call now,' she said as she showed him out.

'Thanks. Bye.'

She picked the phone up and dialled Ted's number. He perked up when he heard her voice and she too felt some comfort from speaking to him. After the pleasantries were over, she continued. 'Ted, I think it would be a good idea if you went up to the house. DI Allix has just left here and is on his way to see Sir Geoffrey.'

'Why? What's wrong?' his voice filled with concern.

'I can't say, it's best if you hear it from DI Allix. Just go and be with Sir Geoffrey and Lady Susan. They're going to need your moral support. Don't worry, he's not going to be arrested or anything.'

'You sure? I'd best get up there then. Speak to you later. Bye.'

Next, Katherine phoned Libby and asked her simply to come over. Without questioning the reason why, Libby arrived an hour later, having left the children with James as soon as he got back from work.

Katherine spent the evening pouring her heart out to Libby, trying to cleanse herself of the horrors of the day. Libby was astounded and horrified, but comforted her friend as best she could, leaving her in a better state than when she arrived. Ted phoned later in the evening, in a state of shock himself about what had happened, to see how Katherine was. Having reassured him that she was fine she took a long hot bath, tucked herself up in bed and immersed herself in her book – A Christmas Carol – removing herself from the present reality.

After a fitful night's sleep, Katherine reluctantly drove herself down to the police station and spent a lengthy while giving her statement. When she appeared into daylight again, the grey cloud had dispersed and the sun was trying to peep through. She took a deep, long, breath and exhaled slowly, clearing her mind. In some way, though the horrors of the previous day and weeks and months were still with her, and would be for some time to come, she felt that she could start to move on. The only thing which still worried her was the thought of Robert Codell and whether he had had a sexual relationship with Cecilia. There was nothing more she could do, it was in the hands of the police and she trusted DI Allix to persevere until he was satisfied that Robert was innocent or not.

Feeling the urge to be around normal people, people carrying on with their everyday lives with nothing as dramatic as what she had experienced going on in their lives, she drove to the town of Tenterden and wandered round the shops, dipping in and out, absorbing the normality of life going on around her. She stopped and had a cappuccino in a small delicatessen and flicked through one of the newspapers provided for customers, drifting into and out of other people's conversations, snippets here and there, all mundane stuff. Revived from her drink she decided to brave Waitrose and do her Christmas food shop so that she need not go near a supermarket for the next week or so. With only two whole days left until Christmas Eve there was a frenzy of buying going on, it was trolley to trolley in the aisles, Katherine hadn't expected it to be quite so busy, having assumed that the manic buying would start at the weekend. It always left her feeling slightly sick at the sight of other people's trolleys at that time of year, people seemed to go to extremes of excess, gorging themselves as though they had never been fed and didn't know where their next meal was going to come from, she winced at the thought of the waste which would be left, perfectly good food which would simply be thrown out, it was disgraceful really.

She told herself to stop moralizing and get off her high horse and battled her way round, doing her best to keep a smile on her face and remain polite, despite other harried and hassled shoppers. She had already ordered a turkey and some sausages and bacon from the village butcher and was going to collect them on Saturday and drop them off at Libby's. It was her contribution to the meal and despite Libby's protests that she need not do it, she had insisted and would drop them off to give Libby plenty of time to do whatever preparations she had in mind.

Feeling as though she had just done ten rounds in a boxing ring, Katherine wearily drove home, her mood lowering as her blood sugar level dropped, knowing that she needed food to boost her. She left all but the frozen and chilled food in their bags on the kitchen floor to be packed away later and flopped on the sofa with a glass of water and her seasonal sandwich of turkey and cranberry sauce which she had purchased from the supermarket. She dozed off and started when there was a rap on the door, feeling slightly confused and dazed, it took her a few moments to come too, noticing with relief that it was still light outside and she hadn't been asleep for hours. A quick glance at her watch told her only an hour had passed, to be precise.

She opened the door rubbing her eyes and was greeted by a huge bunch of red roses. Ted's face peeped round the edge of them. She smiled broadly.

'Hello! Come in,' she was delighted to see him.

'I thought these might cheer you up, you know, what with all you've been through,' he looked worriedly at her.

'That's so kind of you. Thank you, they're beautiful!' She took them from him and he followed her into the kitchen, stepping round the remainder of the as yet unpacked shopping. She searched around for a vase and then realized they were all still packed, improvising she took out a large, and quite elegant, glass jug and arranged the roses in them, they looked perfect. 'I can't remember the last time someone bought me flowers, they're gorgeous, thank you,' she kissed him shyly on the cheek and he grinned at her. He made her feel like a teenager again.

'Good, I'm glad. From what DI Allix said, you had quite an eventful day yesterday.'

'That's an understatement! It's not one I *ever* want to repeat. How are Sir Geoffrey and Lady Susan?' she asked with genuine concern.

His face clouded momentarily. 'Shocked, but at least they know. They were coming to terms with the fact that his baby was dead, but to be told that his baby was murdered by the father of the mother of his child, and that the very same person had been abusing his daughter and was someone who had lived in the village for a long time, and was deemed a respectable member of the community, was beyond belief. They look so dazed and bewildered, so vulnerable, I've never seen them like that before, it's really taken it out of them and of course they still don't know what will happen to Sir Geoffrey, whether he will be charged or not and they're fearful of the reaction from the village. Fortunately they are going away for Christmas and New Year, they're going to her brother and his family for Christmas and then to some friends in the south of France for New Year. It should give them time to start to get their heads around what has happened and hopefully get a boost in support from their friends and family before it becomes public knowledge.'

'I do feel sorry for them. I've become kind of fond of them, I suppose because I've caught a glimpse of the tenderness they have for one another and the fact that, despite appearances and brusqueness, they are very kind and caring people. What he did was so wrong, sex with an under aged girl and on top of that, cheating in a marriage is a big no no as far as I am concerned ...'

'I can understand why,' he murmured remembering what she had told him about her ex-husband.

'To do it with an under aged girl – even a consenting one - is disgusting even though he genuinely had no idea she was under aged. I know it's no excuse, but so many teenage girls do look years older than they really are which is a danger in itself. It's not too difficult to see how he misjudged her age, perhaps out of naivety, I doubt he's had much to do with teenage girls or the younger generation in general. He's not like her father who deliberately had sex with her by forcing himself onto her, it's not like he had a sick incestuous relationship with her.'

'I agree, nothing is ever black and white. It's in no way right what he did, but compassion needs to come into this. I'm just not sure how much of that compassion is going to be shown to them,' he looked grim.

They sat thoughtfully for a while, having moved from the kitchen to the sitting room with their mugs of tea. Katherine was beginning to feel that she was going to be awash with tea the amount she'd recently been drinking.

'Anyway,' he started brightly, 'you're off to Libby's for Christmas then.'

She smiled at the thought of Henry and Alice and the huge excitement and anticipation they would be filled with on Christmas Eve and then Christmas Day. 'I'm looking forward to it, the children are so sweet, I'm staying over that night and coming back on Boxing Day. Means I can have a glass of bubbly without worrying about driving. Tell you what, if I had ever been a drink driver I would never want do it again having seen Rupert. But let's not talk about him anymore. You're off to your brother's house aren't you?'

He grinned. 'Yup, can't wait, going on Saturday and coming back the following Wednesday. Quick days work on Thursday to check the Estate and then I'm off until after New Year. What are you doing at New Year?'

She shrugged. 'Don't know, haven't thought that far ahead. How about you?'

'I've been invited to dinner at a friend's house, think there are going to be about thirty of us. Would you like to come? They are always hopeful that I will bring someone with me, think they might be shocked if I do!'

She blushed, it seemed as though the kernel of a relationship might be growing. 'I'd love to. It'll save them playing matchmaker for you,' she grinned.

Chapter Twenty-Four

Six months later and it was moving in day. Previous days of torrential rain had given way to a soft, warming late spring sunshine. Katherine was up early, she'd spent the previous week cleaning the farmhouse from top to bottom and with Ted's help ferried the boxes with kitchen utensils, crockery and an assortment of other bits to the farmhouse. The boxes were unpacked and the kitchen was ready, it was everything else which remained to be transported from one house to the other and then unpacked.

Katherine had hired a local firm who had promised to arrive at 8 a.m., by 7 a.m. she was itching for them to arrive, eager to get the move going and finally settle into her new house. Dougie and the builders were still at the farmhouse, laying a terrace, rebuilding the tumbledown brick outhouse which she would use as a garden store, then they would move on to building a new two bay, oak-framed cart shed which would serve as a garage and finally, once that was complete, they would lay the drive and redo the fencing, it would be autumn before she finally had the place all to herself, but she didn't mind, it would be comforting to have other people around whilst she settled in.

Fortunately for Katherine the removal men turned up on time and before too long the boxes and her furniture were loaded up to accompany what she had had in storage, which had already been loaded into the van before they arrived at Katherine's rental house. She still had a week left on the rental of the terrace and was leaving the cleaning of it until nearer the hand over date. She slammed the door behind her and jumped into her car, having made quite sure that the removal men knew where to go, she didn't want a last minute hitch.

She led off, constantly checking that they were behind her and a few minutes later they arrived at the farmhouse. It took several manoeuvres for the driver to reverse the van into the drive but within minutes the four men were swarming like worker bees, whizzing boxes and furniture into the house. Each box had been labelled with the room name it was to go to and Katherine went round ticking them off her list. Her furniture was next but it looked sparse in what was a vast space compared to what she was used to. She was impatient to start ordering new furniture but had restrained herself, for it would only be once she was settled into the house and really living in it, that she would truly know what she needed and that could differ to what she thought she needed, besides which with a keen eye on the budget and for a bargain, the sales were coming up shortly and she was hopeful that she might pick up some good deals.

She tried not to moan about the muddy footprints the men were depositing on freshly cleaned floors, just another task to add to the long list of things she needed to do. By late lunchtime the men had finished, she waved them off, closed the front door behind her and did a little jig of excitement, punching the air in triumph. She was finally in, despite everything, she'd done it. There was a knock on the door behind her and she assumed that the removal men had forgotten something. It wasn't them, it was Ted holding up a brown paper carrier.

'Lunch,' he announced, smiling broadly at her.

She grinned back, delighted to see him. 'In that case you can come in!' She kissed him softly on the lips. He scooped his free arm around her and squeezed her. Their relationship was developing slowly and growing stronger as each day went past.

'You can be the first to try out my new seats at the centre island, you are honoured!' she joked. The kitchen was stunning; pale limestone tiles of different sizes fitted neatly together on the floor, the cream painted units brought more light to the kitchen and the multicoloured black granite top sparkled as the sun caught different fragments of colour in its rays. There was a pristine white double butler's sink by the window, which afforded a beautiful view of the garden whilst doing the mundane washing up. It all smelled new, clean and fresh and resembled in no way the rubble strewn place of horror where Cecilia and her baby were found. Katherine had kept the lines clear, clean and simple throughout the house. There were no dramatic or violent colours, just pale creams, soft yellows and gentle pale greens. She had used Farrow & Ball paints throughout and was amazed how the paints changed colour in different light, one moment a soft yellow would look just like that and a while later when the sun had moved round or gone in, it looked like a very pale green. It brought an individuality and uniqueness to the simplicity. Apart from the kitchen, larder and laundry room whose floors were covered in the pale limestone tiles, the rest of the floors were covered in wide, pale, oak floorboards. The fireplace in the winter sitting room had been sandblasted, the oak Bressemer beam brought back to life to show off the stunning piece of oak it was and a small wood burning stove placed within the fireplace.

'I'm surprised you managed to get away,' she commented.

'It was Geoffrey who encouraged me to take the time out,' he still marvelled at the change in Sir Geoffrey and Lady Susan. They had been humbled by their experience and even more so when the village found out that he was the father of Cecilia's baby and the implications which came with it. Far from vilifying him and ostracizing the pair of them, they were forgiving and supportive. He had been fortunate to avoid a full blown Crown Court case and both he and Susan had made radical changes to their lives. With there being no doubt that they would never be parents - the hope finally being dashed with the discovery of the dead baby - they moved forward, galvanized into action to make the Estate work and be successful and not be reliant on an offspring to do so. A combination of Ted's ideas and their's were being put into action. For ten years Ted had been coming up with innovative ways to enhance the coffers of the Estate, but they had all been rejected, now they were not only welcomed but encouraged. Events were being organized, the farms were going to be fully utilized and Sir Geoffrey and Lady Susan had announced that fifty percent of any profit would go to charities to support abused children and women. And finally they had insisted that they be referred to as plain Geoffrey and Susan, no use of their titles to be used. A transformation indeed and one which had rejuvenated them, they were more active, more sprightly and used their commanding skills in a positive way.

At Sir Geoffrey's insistence, Tom was contracted to service all the Estate vehicles, his way of attempting to make amends. After initial resistance Tom had accepted, wanting to keep the past in the past and felt he would be a fool to turn down what could, potentially, be a very lucrative contract, he had a wife and child to support, with another baby on the way.

'I trust Andrew's leaving you alone now? He's not exactly number one favourite around the village since the revelation of his plans for the land around here. Don't think he's got a hope of developing it. Can't imagine how it came out?' he grinned at Katherine.

'Quite a surprise eh?' she joked back. Ted had been one of the few she had told in confidence, before finally letting it slip one day at the Farmers Market, within an hour it was all round the village and the forces were being rallied, the 'Battle against The Battle' as it was now being referred to, swept into action.

'I saw Audrey in the deli,' he added.

'How was she? I haven't seen her for a couple of weeks.' An unlikely bond had formed between the two, they were polar opposites in personality, but previous events had given them a link, a weak one, but a bond between them which was growing stronger and a solid friendship was developing. Audrey had thrown herself into work, was taking part in village life and was doing her very best to build a new life for herself.

'She seemed ok, asked after you, said she'd pop up in a few days to see you.'

'Gosh, that's a big step forward, she's not been here since, well, you know...'

'Mmm. When I popped into the shop, Betty was still full of the latest on Robert. That piece is going to play and play.'

Katherine shivered in disgust. An investigation had revealed that he had, indeed, been abusing children. Several girls had come forward dating back over the past twenty years and a case was being made against him. She sincerely hoped that he would be convicted for what he had done but felt dreadfully sorry for his wife Jane, who, like Audrey, had had no idea what her husband had been up to. She had taken indefinite leave from her job at the school and her husband had been suspended, until he was convicted by the courts they could not sack him, but Katherine was aware that even if, by some total miscarriage of justice, he was not found guilty, then he would not work there again, or at any school, she suspected and fervently hoped. She reflected on how many lives had been ruined by his actions. Not just the girls themselves, but their parents and possibly the relationships and future relationships the girls would have throughout their lives.

Whilst they chatted, Ted unpacked the simple lunch of sandwiches, crisps and smoothies which he'd picked up from a nearby deli, whilst Katherine produced plates and glasses.

'My first official meal here since moving in!' She raised her glass and chinked it against Ted's.

'To your new home! May it be filled with many happy years,' he responded.

Katherine smiled and sighed contentedly. Finally she was in her new home, the home of her dreams and whilst she would never forget Cecilia and her baby, it was time to move on, to create a new episode in the history of the house, for she knew that every house had its secrets – good and bad – it was just she had discovered those of the farm-house, when most people never found out. She gazed at Ted and sincerely hoped that he would be a part of the making of the history of her house, that they would have a long term future together. She felt sure that he would never let her down as her ex-husband had, but then, when she had married Rex she had not expected it to end the way that it had. One never knew what the future would bring, life was an adventure and it was time that her life had a positive adventure.

Printed in Great Britain
by Amazon